Animal Inn 3-Books-in-1!

ANIMAL INN
3-Books-in-1!

A Furry Fiasco

Treasure Hunt

The Bow-wow Bus

PAUL DUBOIS JACOBS
&
JENNIFER SWENDER

Illustrated by STEPHANIE LABERIS

ALADDIN

New York London Toronto Sydney New Delhi

This book is a work of fiction. Any references to historical events, real people, or real places are used fictitiously. Other names, characters, places, and events are products of the author's imagination, and any resemblance to actual events or places or persons, living or dead, is entirely coincidental.

ALADDIN

An imprint of Simon & Schuster Children's Publishing Division
1230 Avenue of the Americas, New York, New York 10020
This Aladdin paperback edition October 2017
A Furry Fiasco and *Treasure Hunt* text copyright © 2016 by Simon & Schuster, Inc.
A Furry Fiasco and *Treasure Hunt* interior illustrations copyright © 2016 by Stephanie Laberis
The Bow-wow Bus text copyright © 2017 by Simon & Schuster, Inc.
The Bow-wow Bus interior illustrations copyright © 2017 by Stephanie Laberis
Cover illustrations copyright © 2016 by Stephanie Laberis
All rights reserved, including the right of reproduction in whole or in part in any form.
ALADDIN and related logo are registered trademarks of Simon & Schuster, Inc.
For information about special discounts for bulk purchases, please contact
Simon & Schuster Special Sales at 1-866-506-1949 or business@simonandschuster.com.
The Simon & Schuster Speakers Bureau can bring authors to your live event. For more information or to book an event contact the Simon & Schuster Speakers Bureau at 1-866-248-3049 or visit our website at www.simonspeakers.com.
Cover designed by Jessica Handelman
Interior designed by Greg Stadnyk
The illustrations for this book were rendered digitally.
The text of this book was set in Bembo Std.
Manufactured in the United States of America 0917 OFF
2 4 6 8 10 9 7 5 3 1
Library of Congress Control Number 2017931242
ISBN 978-1-5344-0964-4 (pbk)
ISBN 978-1-4814-6225-9 (*A Furry Fiasco* eBook)
ISBN 978-1-4814-6228-0 (*Treasure Hunt* eBook)
ISBN 978-1-4814-6231-0 (*The Bow-wow Bus* eBook)
These titles were previously published individually by Aladdin.

CONTENTS

A Furry Fiasco

For Jennifer Weltz

PROLOGUE

Ding-dong!

Ding-dong!

Our doorbell is always ringing.

Ding-dong!

Welcome to Animal Inn. My name is Leopold Augustus Gonzalo Tyler. I am a scarlet macaw.

No, I am not the loopy bird you see on that breakfast cereal box. That is a toucan. I am a macaw. Macaws are intelligent and dignified crea-tures. Toucans are clumsy and make a racket.

Our family began with Mom, Dad, me, and our Tibetan terrier, Dash. I suppose I should also mention their human sons, Jake and Ethan.

Five years ago Cassie was born. She's a human girl.

Four years ago we adopted Coco, a chocolate Labrador retriever.

Three years ago Shadow and Whiskers showed up at our door. They are sister and brother cats.

And one year ago Jake and Ethan won Fuzzy and Furry at the school fair. They are a pair of very adventurous gerbils.

We used to live in an apartment in the city. But when kid number three and dog number two joined the family, Mom and Dad bought this old house in the country.

Animal Inn is one part hotel, one part school, and one part spa. As our brochure says, *We promise to love your pet as much as you do.*

Ding-dong!

Would someone please answer the door?

It could be a Pekinese here for a pedicure. A Siamese for a short stay. Or a llama for a long stay. We've even had an otter sign up for swim lessons. It's no wonder the doorbell is always ringing.

On the first floor of Animal Inn, we have the Welcome Area, the office, the classroom, the party and play room, and the grooming room.

Our family, the Tyler family, lives on the second floor. This includes Fuzzy and Furry locked in their gerbiltorium in Jake and Ethan's room. (More about this later.)

The third floor is for smaller animals. Any guest

who needs an aquarium, a terrarium, or a solarium stays on the third floor.

Ding-dong!

Where is everybody?

Maybe they're out in the barn and kennels. That's where the larger animals stay.

Here at Animal Inn we can provide just about any habitat a guest might need. Hot, cold, wet, dry, forest, desert. We've got it all.

"Habitat" is just a fancy word for "home." We recently added a new habitat. The first guest to stay there caused quite a stir.

Let me tell you what happened a few weeks ago. . . .

CHAPTER
1

It began like any other Saturday morning.

Saturday is a busy day at Animal Inn. Mom teaches her Polite Puppies class. Dad and Jake host the Furry Pages. That's when children read aloud to an animal buddy. And there are grooming appointments and usually a birthday party or two.

On this Saturday morning I was on my perch

in the Welcome Area. Dad was tidying up the brochures. Mom was talking on the phone to an old friend from her dog show days.

Suddenly I heard Jake holler from upstairs. "Where could they be?"

"I don't know," shouted Ethan. "They were in the gerbiltorium a minute ago."

Fiddlesticks. Fuzzy and Furry must have escaped again.

Fuzzy and Furry are experts at picking the lock on their gerbiltorium. They usually escape at night, when guests are safely tucked into their cages, crates, tanks, and stalls.

I was a bit worried that Fuzzy and Furry might run into the new guest on the third floor—a boa constrictor named Copernicus.

"Ethan!" Jake shouted. "Start looking!"

"Stop telling me what to do!" Ethan shouted.

"Ethan! Start looking!" Jake shouted again.

"You're not the boss of me!" Ethan shouted back.

Mom rushed up the stairs. Luckily, the gerbils had not bumped into Copernicus. They were found in Jake and Ethan's laundry hamper, fast asleep.

A few minutes later Cassie came downstairs, followed by Coco.

"Princess Coco," Cassie said, "let's go look for fairies."

"Just have Coco back in time for Furry Pages," said Dad. "And careful not to let Shadow out."

Shadow is supposed to be an indoor cat, but she loves to sneak outside. Cassie and Coco are her best chance for a little adventure.

"Dad," Cassie said. "We are princesses. I am *Princess* Cassie, and this is *Princess* Coco."

"My apologies," Dad said, and smiled. He bowed to them. "I'll be in the basement if you need me."

"I can't believe it!" Cassie whispered to Coco as soon as Dad left. "I just can't believe it!"

I perked up my ears. Yes, I do have ears. They're hidden under my feathers.

What was it that Cassie found so unbelievable?

Like many other five-year-old humans, she can get very excited. "I can't believe it!" is one of her favorite things to say.

Pizza for dinner? I can't believe it!

That hermit crab's name is Banjo? I can't believe it!

Coco gave a tremendous shake. Luckily, one of Jake's Saturday chores is sweeping up the Welcome Area. And after any shake by Coco, the Welcome Area can use a good sweep.

"I can't believe it," Cassie said again, and giggled.

She headed back upstairs. Coco started to follow.

"Ahem." I cleared my throat.

Coco got the message. She stopped in front of my perch.

"*What* is going on?" I whispered.

"So . . . ," Coco started, "Mom was on the phone. Then the gerbils got lost. Then Ethan got mad at Jake for being bossy. Then the gerbils got found. Then Cassie and I were princesses. Then we—"

"Not *that*," I interrupted. "What is it that Cassie can't believe?"

"Oh," said Coco. "Cassie can't believe a lot of things. She can't believe it's almost September. She can't believe it might rain today. She can't believe there's mac-and-cheese for lunch. I love mac-and-cheese. Do you like mac-and-cheese, Leopold?"

I knew it had been a mistake to start a conversation

with Coco. "No," I said. "Macaws do not like mac-and-cheese."

"Really?" Coco gasped. "Mac-and-cheese is my favorite. I always hang out under the table on mac-and-cheese day. Cassie has trouble fitting all those little noodles onto her fork. Some fall onto the floor. Yummy!" Coco licked her lips.

This conversation was getting me nowhere. "Never mind," I said.

Coco started for the stairs. "By the way," she said over her shoulder, "did you hear about the wizard who's coming? Cassie can't believe *that* either."

CHAPTER
2

It wasn't long before Whiskers scurried down the stairs.

"This is *Animal* Inn," he said worriedly. "A wizard is not an animal."

Hmm. Here was another pet talking about a wizard. "What are you fretting about?" I asked.

"Haven't you heard? A new guest is coming." Whiskers gulped. "It's a wizard!"

"Did you say 'wizard'?" Shadow asked, popping out from behind the sofa. "That's so cool!"

"I don't think it's cool," said Whiskers. "What if the wizard casts a spell on us? What if it turns us into houseflies or . . . slugs?"

"That would be awesome!" said Shadow.

"No, it wouldn't," Whiskers replied, trembling.

"Little Brother," said Shadow, "don't be such a scaredy-cat."

Ding-dong!

"The wizard is here!" Whiskers screeched. He jumped straight into the air with his fur raised on end.

Shadow snuck back behind the sofa.

Mom and Cassie came downstairs to answer the door. I raised one wing to tell Mom that, yes, Shadow was hiding behind the sofa.

"Thank you, Leopold," she said.

"Thank you, Leopold," I repeated.

Mom smiled. It makes Mom smile when she thanks me and then I thank myself. And I love to see Mom smile. She opened the door.

To my surprise it really was . . .

Not a wizard. It was a puppy.

The puppy was having a birthday party after Polite Puppies class. His family had arrived early to decorate the room with balloons and streamers.

Mom let them in and quickly closed the door. Then she and Cassie led the birthday pup and his family to the party room.

"Good morning, Shadow," Mom called as she passed by the sofa.

"Okay, wise guys," Shadow huffed at us. "Who told her I was hiding here?"

"Let's focus," I said. "When is this wizard supposed to arrive?"

"Soon," said a voice from the stairs. It was Dash.

It's one thing to hear something from goofy Coco or nervous Whiskers. But when Dash says something, it's usually true. He and I have been with the Tylers the longest. He's been their pet even longer than I have.

"This is terrible," Whiskers whimpered.

"We'll be fine," said Dash calmly. "We just need a plan."

"I've got it," said Whiskers. "I'll distract the wizard with a yowl. Leopold, you snatch his wand and fly it to Dash. Dash, you run and bury the wand in the backyard. No more magic."

"But what if the wizard doesn't use a wand?" Shadow asked. "What if he uses only magic words, such as 'hocus-pocus'?"

"Or 'presto,'" said Dash.

"Or 'abracadabra,'" I added.

Just then Jake and Ethan came downstairs.

Dash sat.

Shadow hid.

Whiskers pretended to sleep on the sofa.

And I squawked, "Abracadabra! Abracadabra!"

"That's a new one, Leopold," said Ethan. He went to join Mom and Cassie for Polite Puppies.

"Come on, Dash. Come on, Leopold," said Jake. "It's time for us to get ready for Furry Pages."

"Listen," Dash whispered to me on the way to the classroom. "I'm telling only *you* this. I don't want to get the others all worked up."

"What is it?" I asked.

"I overheard the boys talking. The wizard is not the guest," Dash said. "The wizard is the owner."

"The owner of what?" I asked. "An owl? A bat?"

"No," whispered Dash. "A dragon."

CHAPTER
3

"Maybe they were talking about

a *make-believe* dragon," I said.

"I don't think so," whispered Dash. "I heard Dad say we need an extra fire extinguisher. And you know what kind of animal breathes fire."

"Fiddlesticks," I said. "This isn't good."

As the children arrived, they arranged their carpet squares on the floor. Jake passed out books to the children who were already sitting.

"We really need a plan," said Dash. "First step, we need information."

"Good morning, everyone," Jake announced. "Welcome to Furry Pages."

Dad hurried into the classroom. "Sorry I'm late," he said.

"We'll have to talk more later," Dash whispered. He headed to an empty carpet square.

Today's books were from the Henry and Mudge series. Henry is a small boy. Mudge is his big dog.

Everybody wanted to sit with Dash. He let himself be patted and pet as the children read. You would never know that he had dangerous dragons and wizards on his mind. Maybe the stories were helping him forget.

I made my best attempt to bark like a dog. A young boy with a runny nose and a determined look came over. He had a copy of *Henry and Mudge and the Happy Cat*.

The story is about a stray cat that shows up at Henry and Mudge's door. The book took me back to the day when Shadow and Whiskers showed up on our doorstep.

"And speaking of big, lovable dogs," Jake announced. "Here's Coco."

Coco lumbered into the room.

"Better late than never," I squawked out loud. Everybody laughed.

Coco is *never* on time. And she can never sit still. Furry Pages is a challenge for her. She usually comes late, leaves early, and naps in between.

Coco flopped down onto an empty carpet square. A couple of the kids who had been reading with Dash moved over to her. Within a few minutes I could hear her softly snoring. Well, I guess that *is* the sign of a good bedtime story.

While the kids read, the parents chatted quietly. Jake passed out people snacks and dog snacks, too.

He helped children sound out difficult words.

I couldn't understand how Jake could be so calm. Wasn't he nervous about the new guest?

"Was that the doorbell?" Dad asked. *He* seemed nervous.

"I didn't hear anything," said Jake.

Dad pulled a crumpled to-do list from his back pocket. He checked it. He checked his watch. He checked the clock on the wall. He checked his list again. He checked—

Ding-dong!

Dad jumped.

"That's *definitely* the doorbell," he said. "Jake, you're in charge. It must be the supplies for you-know-who!"

I looked at Dash. Dash looked at me.

"I hope I didn't forget anything," said Dad,

checking his list again. "Fire Chief Morales will be here this afternoon to inspect the basement."

Basement? What was happening in the basement?

"Relax, Dad," Jake said, and smiled.

Relax? I thought. Was this really a time to relax?

"We need to be extra safe," said Dad. "We need to make sure everything meets fire code."

"I know," said Jake. "But what are the chances that our new guest is *actually* going to breathe fire?"

A guest that breathes fire?

Gulp.

CHAPTER
4

After Furry Pages, I flew back

to the Welcome Area. My mind was fluttering faster than my wings. I could barely hear myself think.

Yip! Yip! Yap! Yap! Yap!

Puppies, puppies, and even more puppies were arriving for the birthday party.

Yap! Yap!

Mom, Ethan, and Cassie were doing their best to guide the guests into the party room.

I settled on my perch. When I looked down, one of the puppies was gnawing on my wooden post.

"Young fellow," I said, "would you please stop?"

The gnawing continued. I let out a loud squawk. That did the trick. The puppy ran off to join the others.

Whiskers jumped down from his spot on the sofa. "What are we going to do, Leopold?" he asked nervously.

"Dash and I are working on a plan," I assured him.

Whiskers buried his head in his paws. "Let's just hide," he said.

"Why hide?" said Shadow, popping out from

behind the sofa. "This place could use some real excitement."

At the moment it seemed plenty exciting to me. A puppy party is a noisy party. I looked over to the party room. Mom was fixing some streamers that had fallen down. Ethan was organizing a game.

When Cassie wasn't hugging the party guests, they were tearing around the room. They sniffed and investigated everything—the treats table, the presents table, the box of supplies for Pin the Tail on the Kitty. They looked like a pack of very small, four-legged detectives.

Detectives! That was what we needed.

Dash came into the Welcome Area from Furry Pages after the last child had left.

"I know who can help us gather information," I said excitedly. "Follow me to the gerbiltorium!"

Dash and I raced up the stairs. We went straight to Jake and Ethan's room. The coast was clear.

"Hi, Dash," said Fuzzy.

"Hi, Leopold," added Furry. "What's up?"

"We've got a job for you," I said. "But it could be dangerous."

"'Danger' is our middle name," said Fuzzy. He was crunching on a piece of celery.

"What's in it for us?" added Furry.

"Two dog biscuits," said Dash.

"They need to be whole," said Fuzzy.

"No crumbs," added Furry.

"Deal," said Dash.

"You won't be disappointed," said Fuzzy.

"We're the best in the business," added Furry.

"But you don't even know what the job is yet," I said.

"Doesn't matter," said Fuzzy. "'Danger' is our first name."

"I thought 'Danger' was your middle name," Dash said.

"Well, actually, 'Danger' is our last name," said Furry.

"It is?" said Fuzzy. "I thought our last name was 'Tyler.'"

"Guys," said Dash, "let's focus. We need you to sneak down to the basement. Then report back to us. Tell us everything you see and hear."

"We're depending on you," I said. "This can't fail."

"'Can't fail' is our middle name," said Fuzzy.

"We have lots of middle names," added Furry.

"My full name," Fuzzy said, "is actually Fuzzy Danger Can't Fail Tyler."

"See, Leopold. You're not the only one with a long, fancy name," added Furry.

They both giggled and began to pick the lock on the gerbiltorium.

CHAPTER
5

Dash and I made our way downstairs.

Whiskers was back on the sofa. He looked even more worried than before.

The front door was wide open, and there was a truck in the driveway. Dad was helping a delivery person unload boxes onto a dolly. There was a light rain, so the boxes were covered with a tarp.

"That's strange," said Dash. "We don't usually get deliveries on Saturday."

"What do you think it is?" I asked.

Shadow slunk out from behind the sofa. "Only one way to find out," she said. She started for the open door.

"Don't go near that truck, Shadow," Whiskers begged. "Remember what happened last time?"

"True," said Dash, "but more information could be helpful."

"I'll be fine, Whiskers," Shadow said. And she slipped out the door.

"Everything is going downstairs," Dad said, wiping off his wet boots. He crossed the Welcome Area and opened the basement door for the delivery person.

I flew over to my perch. Out the window I could

see Shadow sitting in the driver's seat of the delivery truck.

"Can you see her, Leopold?" Whiskers asked.

I nodded. "Same as last time. Paws on the steering wheel."

"Let's hope the keys aren't in the ignition this time," Dash said.

Dash came over and placed his two front paws on the windowsill. We both watched as Shadow scampered from the driver's seat into the back of the truck.

"Best party ever!"

It was Coco, stumbling in from the party room. She had cake frosting all over her snout. "Hey, what are you guys looking at?" She came over next to Dash.

"It's Shadow." I pointed with one wing. "She's in that truck."

"Ooh," said Coco. "She's going to get in trouble."

Dad and the delivery person came up from the basement. Dash quickly took his paws off the windowsill.

"Well, nothing's getting out of there," said the delivery person, pointing downstairs.

"Hope not," said Dad.

"Good luck," said the delivery person. He left and shut the front door.

"Plus," Dad said to himself, "it's too late to turn back now."

Too late to turn back? I thought.

I looked at Dash. He looked as worried as I felt.

Dad headed back down to the basement.

Dash put his paws back up onto the windowsill to check on Shadow. But before he could spot her, a dozen puppies bounded out of the party room.

Yip! Yip! Yap! Yap! Yap!

The party was officially over. Jake, Ethan, and Cassie were making sure every guest had a goody bag.

Yap! Yap!

Mom opened the front door. As the gaggle of puppies bounced out, Shadow snuck back in.

"How about some lunch?" Mom asked the kids.

"Sounds great," said Ethan. "I'm so hungry, I could eat a puppy treat."

The Tylers headed upstairs.

"Shadow! What a relief. You're safe." Whiskers sighed.

"For now," said Shadow. She looked more than a little worried.

"What do you mean?" Whiskers asked.

Shadow looked around nervously. "There were

lots of boxes in that truck." She shivered.

I held my breath.

"Some of the boxes were labeled *Exotic Animal Supplies.*"

"What does 'exotic' mean?" asked Coco.

"It means 'unusual,'" I said.

"Or 'from a different land,'" added Dash.

"Well, that doesn't sound too bad," said Coco.

"It's not," said Shadow. "But some of the boxes were labeled *Dangerous-Animal Containment System.*"

"Did you say . . . 'dangerous'?" Whiskers trembled.

"I don't get it," said Coco. "Why would a wizard need a containment system?"

"I don't think it's for the wizard," I said.

"Then who's it for?" asked Shadow.

I looked at Dash. Dash looked at me. He let out a long sigh.

"Don't panic," he said, "but the wizard is dropping off a dragon."

"A dragon!" shrieked Whiskers.

Ding-dong!

This time we all jumped.

Ding-dong!

Dad ran up from the basement. He opened the door.

A very tall man stood dressed in full firefighting gear. He looked like he had just put out a fire.

CHAPTER
6

"Welcome, Fire Chief Morales," Dad

said.

"Sorry I'm late," said the fire chief. "We were putting out a small brush fire."

"No problem," said Dad. "Thanks for coming on a Saturday. Our special guest arrives tomorrow."

I shivered. The dragon was coming *tomorrow*?

"Let's make sure everything is as safe as possible," said the chief. "Can I see the room?"

Dad led the fire chief down to the basement.

Dash and I looked at each other with alarm. I could see he was shaking.

"What's everybody looking at?" asked Fuzzy and Furry. They poked their heads out of a heating vent in the Welcome Area. They looked a little dusty, but otherwise they were fine.

"What did you find out?" Dash asked.

"We had a few close calls," said Fuzzy.

"*Very* close," added Furry.

"Dad keeps coming downstairs," said Fuzzy.

"He's very nervous," added Furry.

"He almost stepped on us!" said Fuzzy.

"Twice!" added Furry.

"Guys," I said, "just tell us what you found out."

But before the gerbils could answer, I heard Jake shout from upstairs. "Where could they be? Start looking, Ethan!"

"Stop telling me what to do!" said Ethan.

"Start looking!" said Jake.

"You're not the boss of me!" shouted Ethan.

"Uh-oh," said Fuzzy. "I think we're in trouble."

"We'd better get back to the gerbiltorium," added Furry.

They disappeared into the heating vent. Dad and the fire chief came back upstairs.

"Thanks again," said Dad.

"Don't mention it," said Chief Morales.

"I was a little worried," said Dad.

"You did a great job. The new room is officially

up to safety code. But *please* be careful."

My ears perked up. Did he say "new room"? Did he say "be careful"?

Dad waved good-bye to Chief Morales. Then he headed straight back to the basement.

We all waited a moment. Then we quietly made our way toward the stairs. Dash stopped to collect some dog biscuits he had hidden under the sofa.

We went straight to Jake and Ethan's room. All except for Coco.

"Where are you going?" Dash asked her.

"My tummy tells me it's lunchtime," said Coco. "I'm going to find Cassie."

Fuzzy and Furry were already back, snug in their gerbiltorium.

"Report, please," Dash said.

"There's a new enclosure," Fuzzy said.

"It takes up one whole side of the basement," Furry added.

"It's big," Fuzzy said.

"Very sturdy," Furry added.

"It has sand and stones," Fuzzy said.

"Real stones," Furry added.

"There are two heat lamps," Fuzzy said.

"Very toasty," Furry added.

"There's a humidifier to keep the air moist," Fuzzy said.

"Like a jungle," Furry added.

"There's a new fire extinguisher," Fuzzy said.

"And a big first aid kit," added Furry.

"That's all we've got so far," Fuzzy said.

"But we are a little hungry," Furry added.

"Excellent job," I said.

Dash slipped the two dog biscuits through the bars of the gerbiltorium. "They're whole," he assured them. "No crumbs."

Fuzzy and Furry took a couple of bites.

Then they quickly buried the rest under the cedar shavings for later.

"Okay," said Dash. "What does this new information tell us?"

"The new guest needs a lot of space," I said.

"It likes heat and humidity," said Shadow.

"It needs to be separated from the other animals," Whiskers said, trembling, "which means it's *not* friendly."

"It might be friendly," said Dash.

"Then why do we need a first aid kit?" asked Whiskers.

"And a fire extinguisher?" asked Shadow.

"The dragon is going to burn down Animal Inn!" shrieked Whiskers.

"Let's stay calm," I said. "What if we give it a safe place outside where it can breathe its fire?"

"That sounds like a good plan," said Dash. "Like a campfire. Coco and I can collect wood on our afternoon walk."

"Wood for what?" asked Coco, coming in from lunch. She still had some mac-and-cheese on her nose.

"A special campfire," said Dash.

"Oh, goody," said Coco. "Will there be marshmallows?"

CHAPTER
7

Back in the Welcome Area, Cassie

put on Dash's leash.

Shadow rubbed against Cassie's leg.

Mom put on Coco's leash.

Shadow rubbed against Mom's leg. Shadow knows how to make a point.

"Okay, Shadow," Cassie said. "Mom, can Shadow come with us?"

Mom smiled. "Of course. Sometimes I think she's more dog than cat."

Cassie put on Shadow's leash. Yes, Shadow has a special cat leash.

Mom grabbed a big umbrella.

Ding-dong!

Mom opened the door. It was Martha, one of the Animal Inn groomers. While all of our groomers are excellent, Martha is my favorite. I just love the way she trims and files my toenails.

Yes, I have toenails. You might call them talons.

"Hi, Martha," Mom said. "Come on in. Cassie and I are taking the dogs out for a walk."

Shadow gave a loud meow.

"Correction," said Mom. "Cassie and I are taking the dogs and *Shadow* out for a walk. Then we'll check on the guests in the barn and kennels."

"Have fun," said Martha.

I watched as the group of walkers left through the front door.

"Hi, Leopold!" Martha waved. "How's my pretty bird?"

Did Martha know about the dangerous dragon? Would she have to groom its scales and trim its claws? A shiver ran down my back.

Ding-dong!

I froze in place. It's what we macaws do when we're scared.

Martha opened the door.

It was only Monsieur Petit, here for his weekly styling appointment. Monsieur Petit is a miniature French poodle. He is also one of my dearest friends. Monsieur has been coming to Animal Inn every Saturday since the day we opened.

"See you in an hour!" said Monsieur Petit's owner, Madame Gigi.

Then the phone rang.

"Be right back, Monsieur," Martha said, hurrying to the office.

"*Bonjour*, Leopold," Monsieur Petit crooned. "It's wonderful to see you."

I stayed frozen in place.

"What's the matter, *mon ami*?" Monsieur asked.

"We are expecting a new guest," I said. "A strange and scary guest."

"Scary?" Monsieur Petit asked. "Are you sure?"

"I'm not sure of anything," I said.

Monsieur Petit smiled. "This reminds me of a story," he said. "When I was a pup in Paris,

I heard some friends talking about a terrible creature. They said it had horns and wings. I was so scared. And then one day I looked up and I saw the terrible creature perched high above."

Monsieur Petit paused for a moment. I held my breath.

"It really was fierce and frightening," he said slowly.

"Oh dear," I gasped.

"But it was not dangerous." Monsieur Petit smiled. "It was a gargoyle. You do know, *mon ami*, what is a gargoyle?"

"Of course," I said. "It's a stone statue that guides rainwater away from a building."

"Correct," said Monsieur Petit. "I had nothing to fear. Perhaps you do not either."

"Ready, Monsieur?" Martha was back from the office. "Sorry to make you wait."

Monsieur Petit bowed to me, and then followed Martha to the grooming room.

I thought about what my wise friend had said.

Then I heard the sound of hammering. Dad was still working downstairs.

Unfortunately, he was not getting the basement ready for a gargoyle.

CHAPTER 8

"Looks like a storm is coming,"

said Jake as he came downstairs. The clouds were

dark. The rain was now falling steadily.

Jake headed to the supply closet and grabbed

the broom. Dragon or no dragon, there were still

chores to be done.

"Want to help, Leopold?" Jake asked.

I flew over and took my place on Jake's shoulder.

Sweeping with Jake always calms me. He took me for a little ride around the Welcome Area. It felt safe.

Jake was careful not to get too close to Whiskers on the sofa. Brooms make Whiskers nervous. And Whiskers was nervous enough already.

"Come on, Jake," Ethan called from upstairs. "Time for chores."

"I know," Jake called back. "I'm sweeping the Welcome Area."

Ethan came down and slumped on the last stair. "I don't feel like doing chores today," he said.

"I know," said Jake, "but there are about a dozen guests on the third floor. I can't clean, feed, and water them all by myself."

"Why can't Cassie help?" asked Ethan.

"Cassie is helping Mom."

"Well, where's Dad?" Ethan said.

"Dad is busy finishing the new habitat," said Jake. "Aren't you excited about tomorrow? This is a big deal for Animal Inn."

"Yeah," said Ethan, "but new guests mean even more chores."

"Leopold is a pretty bird," I said. I wanted to cheer Ethan up.

I know what it feels like to be the middle child. Dash is older than me. Dash is the leader. Everybody looks up to Dash. Coco is younger than me. Coco gets to goof around, and everybody thinks she's adorable.

"Leopold is a pretty bird," I tried again.

"Hi, Leopold," Ethan said. He patted his knee. This was an invitation for me to go over.

"You want to come upstairs and help us with chores?" Ethan asked.

"Better late than never," I squawked.

"I guess that means yes," said Ethan.

We all headed up to the Reptile Room.

Chore number one—the Turtle Enclosure.

A box turtle named Bert was spending the week with us. His family was backpacking. No turtles allowed.

You might think that a box turtle would be staying in a box. But there you would be wrong. Box turtles are called "box turtles" because they can pull their heads, tails, and legs into their shells, and then close up like a . . . box. This is how they protect themselves in the wild.

Bert is lucky, I thought. *He has a built-in hiding place.*

Inside the turtle enclosure there was moss and ground-up tree bark. Ethan used a spray bottle to mist the moss with warm water, while Jake cleaned the pool. The pool was actually a paint tray filled with water. But it did the trick. Bert seemed quite pleased with his accommodations.

Then the boys rearranged the hideouts and climbing structures in the enclosure. Finally, Jake gave Bert a plate of worms, chopped spinach, and slightly mushy strawberries. Not my cup of tea, but Bert seemed to enjoy it.

Chore number two—the Snake Enclosure.

We moved on to Copernicus, the boa constrictor. He was curled up in his hiding box, taking an afternoon snooze. The snake enclosure was similar to the turtle's, just much bigger. Copernicus is almost five feet long.

Would he be in danger too when the dragon got here?

Outside, there was a rumble of thunder.

"Here comes the storm," said Jake.

Ethan checked the temperature and humidity in the enclosure. Jake made sure Copernicus had plenty of water. They didn't have to feed him, though. He had eaten just before he'd arrived. He wouldn't need another meal for a week.

Good thing too. A boa constrictor's favorite food is mice. And right next door, four generations of the Field family were enjoying a reunion.

Chore number three—the Rodent Room.

The Rodent Room is equipped with a system of tubes and tunnels. The pieces can be connected or disconnected, depending on how many different guests we have. There are wheels and swings and all kinds of toys. It can be a lively place.

Jake and Ethan filled the food bowls and water bottles.

What would a dragon do with a room full of mice? I shuddered at the thought.

Chore number four—the Small Mammal Room.

Our guests at the time included an Angora bunny named Juniper, a guinea pig named Squeaky, and a pair of ferrets named Frank and Bob. They each had their own hutch, except for the ferrets. They were bunking together.

Jake and Ethan scooped out the old cedar shavings. Then they sprinkled in new shavings. Once again they filled the food bowls and water bottles.

"Are we done yet?" asked Ethan. "This is taking forever."

I agreed. I needed to see if Dash was back.

"Almost done," said Jake. He swept up the

shavings that had fallen onto the floor. "You think this is tough. Just wait until tomorrow. That dragon is going to be a ton of work."

"Yeah," said Ethan. "But Dad will do most of it. He said we can't get too close because of the poison spit."

Poison spit? I gulped.

BOOM!

A clap of thunder shook the walls. Lightning flashed outside the windows. Rain poured down.

"Dragon spit is *not* poisonous," Jake said.

Thank goodness! I breathed a sigh of relief.

"It's *toxic*."

CHAPTER
9

Toxic spit! Things were only getting worse.

I flew downstairs to see if Dash, Coco, and Shadow were back.

They barreled through the front door, startling Whiskers, who was still on the sofa. Mom and Cassie quickly undid the leashes and went upstairs to change into dry clothes.

"So much for our plan," said Dash. "Not exactly campfire weather. Maybe the rain will dampen the dragon's fire."

I wanted to tell Dash that fire wasn't our only problem, but everyone looked frazzled. They didn't need to know about the toxic spit just yet.

"Did you gather any wood?" I asked. "In case the rain stops."

"No," Dash said. "There were ... complications."

"Coco got in trouble," said Shadow.

"I only wanted to play with the squirrel," said Coco. "I thought it was Curtis. Remember Curtis, who stayed with us that time? This squirrel looked just like Curtis."

"He looked *nothing* like Curtis," said Shadow. "Curtis was a red squirrel. The squirrel you were chasing was clearly a gray squirrel."

"I still think it was Curtis," Coco said.

BOOM!

Thunder stopped the argument.

BOOM! BOOM!

"We need a new plan," said Dash. "What are we going to do?"

"I know what *I'm* going to do," said Whiskers. "I'm going to hide under the sofa."Whiskers jumped down and crawled underneath.

"And I know what *I'm* going to do," said Shadow. "The next time that door opens, I'm out of here."

"And I know what *I'm* going to do," said Coco. "*I'm* going to be really friendly and helpful and give the dragon lots of mac-and-cheese. If it's full of mac-and-cheese, it won't have room to eat me. Or I might just hide under Cassie's bed."

"You'll never fit under Cassie's bed," scoffed Shadow.

"If anyone is going to hide under Cassie's bed, it's going to be me," Whiskers piped up. He crawled out from under the sofa. "I call Cassie's room! I think her door has a lock. Doesn't it?"

What was happening to us? It felt like we were falling apart, and the dragon wasn't even here yet.

Just then Fuzzy and Furry popped out of the heating vent.

"Dad's done downstairs," Fuzzy said.

"He's sweeping up," added Furry.

"It looks really cool," Fuzzy said.

"State of the art," added Furry.

"But what are we going to do?" Whiskers trembled.

I looked at Dash. Dash looked at me. We both thought for a moment.

"Perhaps we do nothing," I said. "We trust Mom and Dad's plan."

"Yes," said Dash. "They've never let us down before."

Shadow looked out at the pouring rain. Not the best weather for hitting the open road. "Okay," she said. "I'm in."

"Fine," said Whiskers. "But I still call Cassie's room."

CHAPTER
10

It was Dragon Day.

Mom quietly lifted the cover off my sleeping cage in Cassie's room.

"Good morning, Leopold," Mom whispered. Cassie was still asleep.

Between the raging storm outside and nightmares about dragons, I hadn't slept well.

I stretched my wings. Then I made my way

downstairs to the Welcome Area with Mom.

Animal Inn was very quiet. I looked out the window. Usually this was my favorite part of the day, at least when it was sunny. But today it was wet, windy, and gloomy.

A few minutes later Dash tiptoed down the stairs. He sat beside me and waited for Mom to go into the office.

"I couldn't sleep," I whispered.

"Me either," said Dash.

"I hope Mom and Dad know what they're doing," I said.

"Me too," said Dash.

Dad came downstairs next.

"Good morning, Dash. Good morning, Leopold," he said on his way to the office. "Today is the big day. Is everyone excited?"

Dash wagged his tail, but I could see his heart wasn't in it.

Whiskers came downstairs, pausing on each step. He looked around nervously. "Is it here yet?" he asked.

"Not yet," said Dash.

Whiskers scurried across the Welcome Area and hid under the sofa.

Jake and Ethan came downstairs next.

"Good morning, guys," said Ethan. "Did you hear that thunder last night?"

Jake looked out the window at the rain. "Things could get tricky today," he said. He leaned down to pat Dash's head. "But we'll figure it out, old buddy."

The boys went to the supply closet to get our breakfast ready. The lights flickered on and off.

"Uh-oh," said Jake. "I sure hope the power doesn't go out."

"That would be really bad," said Ethan.

Ethan brought my breakfast right to my perch. "Noble King Leopold," he said, and bowed. "Thy breakfast is served." I didn't feel like eating.

The boys went into the office to find Mom and Dad.

"If only King Leopold had a sword and armor," Shadow said, and then snickered, slinking down the stairs. "He could slay the—"

"Don't say that word!" Whiskers cried from under the sofa.

"What word?" said Coco, close behind Shadow. "You mean dra—"

BOOM!

A crack of lightning lit up the sky outside.

BOOM! BOOM!

"Aaahhh!" Whiskers screamed.

"It's just thunder and lightning," said Dash.

"I can't take one more thing!" whimpered Whiskers.

Ding-dong!

CHAPTER
11

Mom, Dad, Jake, and Ethan hurried

out of the office to answer the door.

Outside was a man dressed in a neon green rain suit. His jacket was crisscrossed with reflective stripes. He almost glowed.

Was this the wizard?

"Good morning," the man shouted over the sound of the rain. He pulled off the hood of his jacket. "I'm Mr. Washburn from the Reptile Rescue Center."

"Rescue?" I said to Dash. "Since when do dragons need rescuing?"

"We're the ones who need rescuing," Whiskers squeaked from under the sofa.

"Please, come in," said Dad.

From my perch I could see a truck in the driveway. There were two other figures dressed in the same neon green suits.

Three wizards?

The two figures were sliding a large, rectangular crate out of the back of the truck. There were lots of small holes along the sides of the crate. It looked like steam was rising off the top.

The two figures started for the front door. Lightning seemed to flash with every step they took.

"Guys," I whispered, "come look at this."

Dash and Coco put their paws on the windowsill. Shadow jumped up too.

"Is that it?" said Shadow. "I thought it would be bigger."

"Maybe it's a baby," said Coco. "I love babies."

"Pretty big baby," said Dash.

BOOM!

Thunder shook the window.

Jake came up behind us. "Hey, guys, I know you're curious to meet our new guest. But let's move away so the handlers can do their job."

I looked at Dash. *"Handlers?"* I said. "Not *wizards?*"

"I'm confused," said Coco.

"Join the club," said Shadow.

Dad held the door open while Mr. Washburn helped the two handlers bring in the crate.

"Where's Cassie?" Jake asked Ethan. "Doesn't she want to see this?"

"I don't know," said Ethan.

Steam was still rising off the crate. The handlers carried it across the Welcome Area, slowly and carefully. Mom opened the basement door.

We all huddled into a corner. Even Shadow was on guard.

"Easy does it," said Mr. Washburn as they made their way down the stairs. "Miss KD has had a long journey."

"Miss KD?" Coco said. "It's a *girl* dragon?"

CHAPTER
12

We heard a rattle in the heating

vent. Out popped Fuzzy and Furry. Even they
looked shaky.

"We were just downstairs," said Fuzzy.

"With the green guys," added Furry.

"What did you find out?" I asked.

"They said it's not full grown," said Fuzzy.

"But it *is* a dragon," added Furry.

"It's the largest kind of dragon in the world," said Fuzzy.

"It's going to get really big," added Furry.

"It can run for short distances," said Fuzzy.

"A real sprinter," added Furry.

"And it eats almost any kind of meat," said Fuzzy.

"Including rodents," added Furry.

"*We're* rodents," said Fuzzy.

"So . . . we'll be in the gerbiltorium," added Furry. They quickly disappeared back into the heating vent.

Just then we heard the strangest noise coming from the basement. It was high-pitched and scary.

"Was that a *roar*?" I asked.

Mom, Dad, Jake, and Ethan were down there!

"We have to help them," said Dash. "First, we all run downstairs. Then Coco and I will growl the dragon into a corner."

"I can help too," said Shadow. She let out a very convincing hiss.

"I'll flap my wings and push the humans upstairs," I said.

"What can I do?" Whiskers asked. He crawled out from under the sofa.

"Very important," said Dash. "As soon as everyone is up here, you slam the door."

But before we could put our plan into action, Mom, Dad, Jake, Ethan, Mr. Washburn, and the two handlers all came up from the basement.

"Everything is great," said Mr. Washburn.

Great? I thought.

"Miss KD will be very happy here," said one of the handlers.

"Thanks," said Dad.

"We're excited to have her," said Mom.

"You have the care instructions," said Mr. Washburn. "Call us if you have any questions. We'll be back as soon as her new home is ready."

Mr. Washburn and the handlers said good-bye and headed for the truck.

"What's going on?" It was Cassie. She was wearing Mom's bathrobe. "Is it here?"

"Why are you wearing a bathrobe?" asked Ethan.

"It's not a bathrobe," said Cassie. "It's a *kimono*. To meet the kimono dragon."

Ethan rolled his eyes. "Cassie, it's a *Komodo* dragon, not a *kimono* dragon."

I looked at Dash. Dash looked at me. "A *Komodo* dragon?" I whispered.

"So where is it?" Cassie asked. "Where's the wizard?"

"Cassie, repeat after me," said Jake. "It's '*lizard*,' not '*wizard*.'"

Cassie tried hard to make the *L* sound, but it still came out sounding like "wizard."

"Wait," whispered Dash. "The wizard is a *lizard*?"

"I want to meet her!" said Cassie.

"Remember," said Dad, "you can visit Miss KD only with a grown-up."

"Let's have some breakfast first," said Mom, "and let Miss KD settle in."

Cassie frowned, but the Tylers headed upstairs.

The basement door was open just a crack.

"Follow me," whispered Shadow. "Let's investigate."

We crept down the stairs. Shadow first, then Dash and me, then Coco, and finally Whiskers.

"Where's the dragon?" asked Shadow.

"I think she's still in the crate," I said.

"Why?" asked Coco.

"Maybe it gives her a place to feel safe," said Whiskers.

Dash tiptoed over to the enclosure. He was cautious at first.

"Come here, guys," whispered Dash. "You'll never believe this."

The dragon was ... *crying*.

That was the sound we had heard before. Our

fire-breathing, rodent-eating dragon was . . . *crying*?

"But why is she crying?" asked Coco. "I'm pretty sure dragons don't cry."

"Maybe she's scared," said Whiskers.

"Don't be scared," I said to our new guest. "We're excited to meet you."

We heard a few more sniffles. "Thank you," she said. "I'm Miss KD." To our surprise, her voice sounded small and frightened.

Suddenly a long yellow tongue appeared from the crate. It was forked at the end. It moved around, as if it were tasting the air.

Miss KD slowly crawled out. I could not connect the frightened voice to the body. Miss KD was as big as Dash. Maybe bigger.

She had a flat head, large claws, and a long tail.

In a word, she was magnificent.

CHAPTER
13

Fuzzy and Furry suddenly popped

out of a heating vent in the basement.

"Are you guys okay?" asked Fuzzy.

"We couldn't find you," added Furry.

"We're fine," I said. I pointed a wing toward the

enclosure. "Let me introduce Miss KD."

"Nice to meet you, my little mouse friends," said

Miss KD.

"Oh, we're not mice," said Fuzzy.

"We're gerbils!" added Furry.

Miss KD seemed a little embarrassed. "My apologies," she said. "I should be more careful, especially since folks are always confusing *me* for something *I'm* not."

"Like a dragon?" asked Shadow.

"Yes, sometimes," said Miss KD.

"Or a wizard?" asked Coco.

"Now, that's a new one." Miss KD smiled.

I cleared my throat. "Maybe I should explain," I said.

I told Miss KD everything that had happened since yesterday. And now it sounded so silly that we all started to laugh.

"It's an easy mistake to make," Miss KD said. "That's why we're called Komodo dragons. When humans first spotted us on the island of Komodo, they thought we *were* dragons. But we're really lizards. The people of Indonesia call us *ora*."

"What's an Indonesia?" Coco asked. "Is it something to eat?"

"Oh, no," Miss KD said, and chuckled. "Indonesia isn't a *what*. It's a *where*. It's a country in Southeast Asia. It's where I come from."

"Then how did you get here?" Shadow asked.

"That is a tale almost as long as my tail," Miss KD said. "But I'm happy to tell it."

We all settled in to hear her story.

"I started as an egg in a clutch on an island called Flores. Luckily, my mother was good at creating decoy nests. I hatched. Believe it or not, I was only thirty centimeters long when I was born."

Coco looked confused.

"About a foot," Dash explained.

"Exactly," Miss KD said. "I spent the first few years of my life high in the trees to avoid predators. When I turned four, I came down to the ground."

Miss KD paused for a moment, as if she were coming to the difficult part of her story.

"Then one day I came face-to-face with a human. He was shaking a big stick at me. I ran in the other direction, but I couldn't get away because he had helpers."

"What happened?" Dash asked.

"The next thing I remember," Miss KD said, "I was in a dark box that was too small for me. There was a loud noise all around, like the buzzing of hundreds of bees. I didn't know it at the time, but I was in an airplane. There were other creatures in cages too—a baby ape, four turtles, and a couple of snakes. We were scared and confused. We had been captured."

"That's terrible," Whiskers said.

"I wound up in Florida," Miss KD said. "It was hot and humid, just like home. But as I grew, my cage got too small. I wasn't getting the right kind of food. I started to get sick."

Miss KD paused and took a deep breath.

"I don't know how it happened, but one lucky day Mr. Washburn showed up with his truck and his friends. They took very good care of me. And now here I am with all of you."

"Welcome to Animal Inn," I said.

EPILOGUE

I learned a lot of important lessons

from Miss KD:

1. Sometimes scary things are not as scary
   as you think.

2. It's better to stick together than fall apart.
   (Especially when you're scared.)

3. Don't believe everything you've heard.
   (Especially if you've heard it from
   Cassie . . . or Coco . . . or Whiskers.)

4. Kimono is something to wear. Komodo
   is somewhere to visit.

One day Mr. Washburn returned to Animal Inn. The Reptile Rescue Center was ready for Miss KD. Like all other Animal Inn guests, Miss KD was moving on.

We promised to keep in touch. But that can be difficult when one of you is a scarlet macaw and the other one is a hundred-pound lizard.

I was settled on my perch in the Welcome Area the next day when Cassie came downstairs. She flopped onto the sofa. I could tell by her red, puffy eyes that she had been crying.

"Leopold, I'm so sad," she said. "I miss Miss KD."

I nodded.

"I know it's not fair to keep some animals as pets," she said, "but I really miss her."

I missed her too.

Then something near the window caught Cassie's attention.

"A butterfly!" she cried. "A real monarch butterfly!"

Cassie jumped up and ran to the door. "Here, little butterfly!" she called.

She ran outside, leaving the door wide open. It was an opportunity too good to miss. Shadow followed close behind. Even Whiskers peeked outside to see what all the excitement was about.

An ocean of orange-and-black wings flew overhead.

Mom ran outside, holding the reservations book.

"They're early," she said to herself. She was trying to hold the big book and turn pages at the same time. "I have them arriving next week."

"Beautiful butterflies!" Cassie called. "Welcome to Animal Inn!"

"Dad! Jake! Ethan!" Mom hollered. "All hands on deck. We have a lot of new guests to check in!"

Treasure Hunt

For Mary Anne A.

PROLOGUE

Ring-ring!

Ring-ring!

Our phone is always ringing.

Ring-ring!

Welcome to Animal Inn. My name is Dash. I'm a Tibetan terrier.

No, I'm not from Tibet. I live in the Virginia countryside. To be honest, I'm not even a terrier.

When people outside of Tibet first saw my ancestors, they thought we looked like terriers.

We Tibetan terriers are shaggy and surefooted. We're known as good luck charms and as excellent companions. This comes in handy because I am a companion to *a lot* of animals and people.

I live with my family, the Tylers—Mom, Dad, Jake, Ethan, and Cassie—plus six other pets:

- Leopold—a scarlet macaw
- Coco—a chocolate Labrador retriever
- Shadow and Whiskers—sister and brother cats
- and Fuzzy and Furry—a pair of very adventurous gerbils

We used to live in an apartment in the city. But when kid number three and dog number two joined the family, Mom and Dad bought this old house in the country.

Animal Inn is one part hotel, one part school, and one part spa. As our brochure says: *We promise to love your pet as much as you do.*

Ring-ring!

Would someone please answer the phone?

It could be a Pekinese for a pedicure. A Siamese for a short stay. Or a llama for a long stay. We even had a Komodo dragon bunk in our basement. But that's another story. It's no wonder the phone is always ringing.

On the first floor of Animal Inn, we have the Welcome Area, the office, the classroom, the party and play room, and the grooming room.

Our family lives on the second floor. This includes Fuzzy and Furry locked in their gerbiltorium in Jake and Ethan's room. (More about this later.)

The third floor is for smaller animals. Any guest who needs an aquarium, a terrarium, or a solarium stays on the third floor.

Ring-ring!

Where is everybody?

I know I have excellent hearing, but am I the only one who hears the phone? Maybe everyone else is out in the barn and kennels. That's where the larger animals stay.

Here at Animal Inn we pride ourselves on calm and comfort. But that was put to the test when we were almost raided by pirates.

Let me tell you what happened. . . .

CHAPTER
1

The day began like any other

Saturday morning.

When I padded downstairs, the sun was just coming up. Mom was already in the Welcome Area with a cup of coffee in one hand and a to-do list in the other.

Leopold was on his perch, his feathers neatly groomed. Leopold always likes to look his best.

"Good morning, Leopold," I said. "Nice day, isn't it?"

"Yes," Leopold agreed. "Nice and quiet."

Dad soon came downstairs with an armload of camping equipment.

"Did you find the poles?" Mom asked him.

Dad held up the tent poles. "Got 'em," he answered. "Are you sure you can manage here alone?"

"I'll be fine," Mom said, checking her to-do list. "It's going to be a quiet day."

I looked at Leopold. Leopold looked at me. Saturdays at Animal Inn are rarely quiet.

In fact, Saturday is our busiest day. Mom teaches her Polite Puppies class. Dad and Jake host the Furry Pages. That's when children read aloud to an animal buddy. Then there are grooming

appointments and usually a birthday party or two.

"I've got it all worked out," Mom began. "Polite Puppies are going to join Furry Pages. That way I can run both programs at the same time. Plus, Mary Anne from the library is coming to give me a hand."

"Sounds like a great plan," said Dad.

My ears perked up. I love when Mary Anne comes to Furry Pages. She always brings cool books from the library.

"We have only one grooming appointment," Mom continued. "Monsieur Petit. Martha will do that. There are no parties, and we're not expecting any new guests."

"You're right," Dad said with a smile. "A quiet day."

I let out a sigh. We needed a quiet day.

The day before, we had said good-bye to 2,311 monarch butterflies. They had been spending a few days at our milkweed patch on their way to Mexico. During the previous few weeks waves of monarchs had been stopping at Animal Inn to relax and recharge.

Suddenly I heard Ethan from upstairs. "Where's *my* sleeping bag?" he hollered.

"I don't know," shouted Jake. "Did you put it in the pile?"

"Where's the pile?" Ethan asked.

"Yeah," chirped Cassie. "Where's the Nile? Is that where we're camping tonight?"

"We're not camping on the Nile," said Ethan. "The Nile is in Africa."

"Ethan!" Jake shouted. "Did you feed Fuzzy and Furry?"

"I thought you fed them!" Ethan shouted back.

Mom looked at Dad. "Are you sure *you're* going to be okay?"

Dad smiled and shrugged. Then he hurried upstairs to help the kids.

A few minutes later Cassie and Coco came downstairs. Shadow followed in their . . . shadow. Shadow is supposed to be an indoor cat, but she loves to sneak outside.

"Don't tell anybody I'm here," Shadow whispered to Leopold and me. She snuck behind the sofa, ready to slip outside if given the chance.

"Princess Coco," Cassie said, pouting. "The campground says no dogs allowed. They're meanies."

"Good morning, Cassie," said Mom. "Are you excited to go camping?"

"Sort of," said Cassie. "I wish Coco could come. Maybe I can dress her up like a person." Cassie took off her jacket and tried to put it on Coco. Coco gave a big shake.

"Coco can help me with Polite Puppies and Furry Pages," Mom said. "Then she and I can take a nice, long afternoon nap." Coco flopped down onto the floor with a sigh.

Dad, Jake, and Ethan came downstairs next. It was difficult to see them through the jumble of camping supplies they carried.

"Better late than never," Leopold squawked.

"Very funny, Leopold," said Ethan.

"Are you sure you'll be able to manage here alone?" Dad asked Mom again.

"Alone?" said Mom with a smile. "I've got Dash, Leopold, Coco, Shadow, and Whiskers."

"And Fuzzy and Furry," added Ethan.

"And don't forget the guests," said Jake. "You've got four frogs, a turtle, and two hamsters on the third floor, an alpaca in the barn, and a cat and three dogs in the kennel."

I had to agree. You're never really alone at Animal Inn.

CHAPTER
2

Loading the car was a bit hectic,

but the campers finally left. The Welcome Area
was quiet again.

"Ah," sighed Mom. She sat down on the sofa.
"A whole weekend to myself."

"Leopold is a pretty bird," Leopold squawked.

"You're right," Mom said with a smile. "I

couldn't forget you, Leopold. Or you, Dash." She gave me a pat on the head.

"There is one thing I need to do," said Mom. "I need to e-mail a coupon to our mailing list—five percent off any Animal Inn service. After that, it's Polite Puppies and Furry Pages, a few chores, and then we can all relax." She stood up and headed for the office.

Maybe this would be a calm Saturday after all. Coco was already asleep on the floor, softly snoring.

"Wow," came a voice from the bottom of the stairs. "It's so peaceful down here today."

It was Whiskers. Whiskers tends to be a little nervous. He made his way across the Welcome Area and happily settled into his usual spot on the sofa.

Ding-dong!

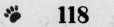

"Who could that be?" asked Mom, coming out of the office. She hurried to answer the front door.

It was Cassie. She looked like she was going to cry.

"What's wrong?" asked Mom. "Did you forget something?"

"I miss Coco," Cassie said with a sniffle. Coco sleepily raised her head.

Mom leaned down and wiped away Cassie's first tears. "It's only for one night, sweetheart," she said.

"I know," said Cassie. "But I want to stay home."

Dad soon followed. He held Cassie's gear under one arm, and Shadow under the other. He shrugged. "One wants to abandon ship. One wants to stow away."

Mom smiled and took Shadow from Dad.

Dad put down Cassie's gear. "Try as I might, I couldn't change her mind," he said.

"It's fine," said Mom. "Cassie can help me here."

Cassie ran over and gave Coco a big hug.

"I guess we'll see you tomorrow," said Dad.

Mom kissed Dad good-bye, put Shadow down, and went back to the office. Cassie stayed glued to Coco.

"Good try," I whispered to Shadow.

Shadow huffed. "I sneezed in the car and gave myself away."

"Well, I'm glad you're back," said Whiskers. "We're going to have a quiet day."

"You mean a *boring* day," scoffed Shadow.

Ring-ring!

Ring-ring!

"Hello. Animal Inn," we heard Mom say from the office. "I'm having trouble hearing you. Can you speak louder? You're at the harbor?"

Whiskers looked up from the sofa.

"Today?" we heard Mom ask. "It is a bit last-minute. What's the guest's name?"

"A new guest?" said Cassie, perking up. She hurried toward the office door. Coco started to follow her.

"Sorry, Coco," Cassie said. "You know the rules. No animals allowed in the office."

Coco flopped back down onto the floor with a sigh.

"The name is Blackbeard?" we heard Mom ask.

"Blackbeard?" Cassie said excitedly. "That sounds like a pirate name." She disappeared into the office.

"Did Cassie just say 'pirate'?" Whiskers asked with a worried look.

"I believe so," said Leopold.

"Awesome!" said Shadow. "Pirates are way cooler than Polite Puppies."

CHAPTER
3

"Hold on," I said. **"Let's not get**
ahead of ourselves. Remember what happened
with Miss KD?"

Miss KD was the Komodo dragon who stayed
in our basement. Before her arrival, there were a
lot of misunderstandings about what she was.

"First we thought she was a wizard," I reminded

Whiskers. "Then we thought she was a real, fire-breathing dragon."

"In the end," said Leopold, "she was a polite guest and a good friend. And we learned not to believe everything Cassie says."

"It's not just what Cassie said," insisted Whiskers. "It's what Mom said. Harbor? Blackbeard? It can mean only one thing."

"A pirate!" cheered Shadow. "To think, a real plank-walking, treasure-seeking, sword-wielding pirate is coming here to Animal Inn."

We actually knew a lot about pirates. Pirate stories were a favorite choice for family movies and Furry Pages.

"Don't pirates have crews?" Whiskers asked worriedly. "What if *lots* of pirates are coming?"

"The more salty dogs the better," said Shadow.

"Salty dogs?" asked Coco, suddenly awake. "Do you eat them with ketchup? Or mustard?"

"Salty dogs are not something to eat," I explained.

"Salty dogs are pirates," said Leopold.

"Pirates?" asked Coco. "Why are we talking about pirates?"

"Haven't you been listening?" Whiskers asked.

"No," said Coco. "I've been napping. I thought we were having a quiet day."

"A last-minute guest is coming," I explained. "The name is Blackbeard."

Ding-dong!

"Batten down the hatches!" Whiskers screeched.

"Shiver me timbers," Shadow said with a grin. She snuck back behind the sofa.

Mom and Cassie came out from the office to answer the door. I pointed with my nose to alert Mom that, yes, Shadow was hiding behind the sofa.

"Thank you, Dash," she said.

To our surprise it really was . . .

Not a pirate.

It was Mary Anne, the librarian.

"Come on in," said Mom, holding open the door.

"Good morning. I brought books for Furry Pages," said Mary Anne. She held out a big bag of books. "Cassie, do you want to help me choose some favorites?"

"Yes," said Cassie. "Can Coco help too?"

"Of course," said Mary Anne.

"I'll join you in a minute," said Mom. "I need to get ready for a last-minute guest."

"It's a harbor pirate," Cassie told Mary Anne.

Mary Anne smiled. "That's exciting," she said.

Cassie and Mary Anne headed to the classroom. Coco followed close behind.

"*See?*" said Whiskers. "It *is* a pirate." He buried

his head under a sofa cushion. "I don't want to walk the plank. All I want is a quiet day."

"It will be a quiet day," I said.

I hoped I was right.

CHAPTER
4

"Good morning, everyone,"
Mary Anne announced. "Welcome to Furry
Pages and Polite Puppies."

As Cassie and Mary Anne handed out books to
the children, the puppies tugged and pulled on the
carpet squares. The puppies were still learning to
be polite.

I had a moment to think. *Why would a pirate*

come to Animal Inn? I couldn't think of any logical reason. Surely we had nothing to worry about.

Cassie brought Coco over to my carpet square so that she could read to both of us.

"I found a pirate book!" she said excitedly. She held up *Eloise's Pirate Adventure.*

It's only a book, I told myself.

Cassie started reading. Soon I could hear Coco softly snoring. Well, I guess that *is* the sign of a good bedtime story.

Mom hurried into the classroom. "Sorry I'm late," she said. She had the phone in one hand and her to-do list in the other.

While the kids read, the parents chatted quietly. Mary Anne passed out puppy snacks, and people snacks too. She and Mom helped the children sound out difficult words.

Soon most of the puppies were snoozing just like Coco. Maybe it would be a quiet day after all.

Ring-ring!

Ring-ring!

"Animal Inn," Mom answered. "Oh, hi again. Yes, we do have parrot food."

Parrot food? I thought.

"Of course," Mom said. "There's plenty of space for Blackbeard to dig."

Did she just say "dig"?

"Can you e-mail me the information?" Mom asked. "I'm sure we'll find a safe place for your treasure."

Treasure!

A pirate is dangerous enough. But a pirate with treasure to hide? Maybe we did have something to worry about after all.

How could Mom be so calm? Wasn't she nervous about the new guest? I hurried to the Welcome Area.

"Leopold," I whispered. "We may have a real problem." I filled him in on what I'd just heard.

"We're going to need assistance," said Leopold. "Follow me to the gerbiltorium."

We rushed up the stairs to Jake and Ethan's room. Fuzzy and Furry were lounging in one of their play structures.

"Hi, Dash. Hi, Leopold," said Fuzzy.

"Care for a snack?" added Furry. He held out a sunflower seed.

"No time," I said. "We need your help."

"It involves computers," said Leopold.

"No problem," said Fuzzy. "You've heard of a computer mouse?"

"We're computer gerbils," added Furry.

"We're very tech-savvy," said Fuzzy.

"But it will cost you," added Furry.

"How many dog biscuits?" I asked.

"Not dog biscuits," said Fuzzy.

"We're talking walnuts," added Furry.

"I can get walnuts," said Leopold.

"Deal," said Fuzzy.

"Give us the details," added Furry.

"We need information about a last-minute guest," I explained. "Your job is to sneak into the office and print out an e-mail."

"Easy," said Fuzzy. "Is the e-mail coming to Mom's address or to Dad's address?"

"Or the general Animal Inn address?" added Furry.

"We don't know," I said. "But look for any message with the word 'Blackbeard' or 'treasure.'"

"Did you say 'treasure'?" asked Fuzzy.

"We are expert treasure-hunters," added Furry.

"We have quite a collection," said Fuzzy.

"We keep it locked in the old chest in the attic," added Furry.

"We recently added a windup mouse and a rubber hot dog," said Fuzzy.

"Would you like to see them?" added Furry.

"Maybe later," I said. "But right now we need that e-mail."

"It's extremely urgent," said Leopold.

"No sweat," said Fuzzy.

"We know all the passwords," added Furry.

They giggled and picked the lock on the gerbiltorium. Then they scampered into the heating vent and disappeared.

CHAPTER
5

Leopold and I rushed back downstairs.

Yip! Yip! Yap! Yap! Yap!

The dismissal of Furry Pages and Polite Puppies was a bit chaotic.

Yap! Yap!

Owners were chasing after puppies. Tail-wagging puppies were chasing after one another.

Mary Anne did her best to hand bookmarks out to the children.

As Mom and Cassie waved good-bye to the last puppy, a few leaves blew into the Welcome Area.

"That was quite a whirlwind," said Mom, shutting the door. Then she, Cassie, and Mary Anne went back to the classroom to clean up. Polite Puppies can make quite a mess.

"All clear," Leopold said from his perch. I nodded and took my position at the office door.

"What's going on?" Whiskers asked from the sofa.

"Fuzzy and Furry are getting information about the last-minute guest," whispered Leopold.

"They're in the office now," I added.

"But I thought there was nothing to worry about," Whiskers said.

"That's what we're trying to find out," I answered.

I listened carefully, my ear to the door. I heard noises coming from inside the office—shuffling and clicking and beeping noises.

"What's Mom's password?" I heard Fuzzy ask.

"Dash-Tibetan-seven," said Furry.

I stood up a little straighter. I hadn't known I was Mom's password.

"Nothing there," said Fuzzy. "What's Dad's?"

"Leopold-macaw-eight," said Furry.

"Nothing there," said Fuzzy. "What about the general Animal Inn address?"

"*J-E-C*-three-*S-W*-two-*F-F*-two," said Furry.

"How do you remember all that?" asked Fuzzy.

"Easy," said Furry. "*J* is for Jake. *E* is for Ethan. *C* is for Cassie. The number three is for three kids. *S* is for Shadow. *W* is for Whiskers. Two is for . . ."

Suddenly I noticed Leopold. He was waving a wing to get my attention.

I quickly stepped away from the office door.

Mom and Mary Anne were coming back into the Welcome Area. Cassie and Coco followed.

"Thanks so much for your help today," said Mom.

"I had a lot of fun," said Mary Anne, waving good-bye.

Mom shut the front door and took out her to-do list. Her next stop would probably be the office.

I looked at Leopold. Leopold looked at me and nodded.

Squawk! Squawk!

Squawk! Squawk!

Hopefully, his squawks sent a clear message to Fuzzy and Furry: *Hurry up!*

I inched closer to the office door. I heard a few more beeps and clicks.

"Say cheese!" said Fuzzy.

"Smile!" added Furry.

I heard a whir, a rip, a double-thump, and a skitter.

"Is it time for lunch yet?" Cassie asked. She flopped onto the floor next to Coco.

"Almost," said Mom. "I just need to e-mail that coupon for five percent off."

I gulped. I sure hoped Fuzzy and Furry were finished.

Ding-dong!

"Now, who could that be?" said Mom.

Whew! I thought. Saved by the bell.

Mom opened the front door. It was Mary Anne with Shadow under one arm.

"I found this stowaway in the back of my pickup truck," Mary Anne said with a smile.

"Sorry about that," said Mom. She took Shadow from Mary Anne. "Twice in one day, Shadow?" she asked, setting her down on the floor. Shadow quickly scampered behind the sofa.

"*Now* is it time for lunch?" asked Cassie.

Mom nodded. "Just need to send the e-mail."

Cassie followed Mom into the office. I held my breath.

"That's odd," I heard Mom say. "I don't remember sending the coupon. But I guess I did. It says right here, 'Message sent.'"

I looked at Leopold. Leopold looked at me.

What had Fuzzy and Furry done now?

CHAPTER
6

Fuzzy and Furry poked their heads out of the heating vent in the Welcome Area. They looked a little bleary-eyed from staring at the computer.

"Thanks for the squawk, Leopold," said Fuzzy.

"We got away just in time," added Furry.

"What did you find?" I asked.

"First," said Fuzzy, "the new computer is awesome."

"It can play music, take pictures, and even show movies," added Furry.

"Second, we found a box of paper clips," said Fuzzy.

"Good for picking locks," added Furry.

"Third, there are new photos on the wall," said Fuzzy.

"There's a nice one of you and Leopold," added Furry.

"And another of Shadow and Whiskers," said Fuzzy.

"And one of Coco eating cheese," added Furry.

"Did someone say 'cheese'?" Coco asked, opening her eyes.

"But there's no picture of us," sighed Furry.

This was typical of the gerbils. They were easily distracted.

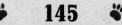

"Guys," I interrupted. "Did you find the e-mail?"

"Oh, we found the e-mail," said Fuzzy.

"We printed it out," added Furry.

"First the paper jammed," said Fuzzy.

"Then it unjammed," added Furry.

"So, where is it?" asked Leopold.

"We have it right here," said Fuzzy. He pulled a crumpled piece of paper out of the heating vent.

"But we didn't have time to read it," added Furry.

"I can read it for you," offered Coco.

"Hang on just a second," said Shadow. She strolled out from behind the sofa. "*You* can read, Coco? When did you learn?"

"Furry Pages," said Coco. "You should join us sometime. It's very educational. I started with

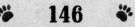

Go, Dog. Go! But you might want to try *The Cat in the Hat*."

Coco took the paper from Fuzzy. She smoothed it out on the floor with her paws.

"It says, 'Overnight delivery *cone*-formation.'" Coco looked up. "What is a *cone*-formation? Is it like an ice-cream cone?"

I looked at the page. I said, "It's not '*cone*-formation.' It's '*confirmation*.' Overnight delivery confirmation."

"What about Blackbeard?" Whiskers asked nervously.

"What about the treasure?" asked Shadow.

I looked at the page more carefully. It had nothing to do with pirates. "This is an e-mail receipt," I said. "It's from a company called Picture *Purr*fect."

"Uh-oh," said Fuzzy. "We may have printed the wrong e-mail."

"We were in a rush," added Furry.

"What now?" asked Whiskers.

I thought for a moment. "As a precaution," I said, "we should have a lookout."

"We can be the lookout," said Fuzzy.

"We're expert lookouts," added Furry.

"To the crow's nest!" said Fuzzy.

"It's a *real* crow's nest," added Furry. They scampered off into the heating vent.

"I can't wait to see the Jolly Roger," said Shadow.

"Jolly?" asked Whiskers. "That doesn't sound scary. And who's Roger?"

"The 'Jolly Roger' is another name for the pirate flag," explained Leopold. "It traditionally features a skull and crossbones."

Whiskers's fur stood on end. "Skulls and bones!" he cried.

"Stay calm," I said. "Let's think. What do we know for certain?"

"We know someone named Blackbeard is coming," said Leopold.

"We know he's coming from the harbor," added Coco.

"We know he has a treasure," said Shadow.

"And we also know pirates carry swords!" cried Whiskers.

"Swords-shmords," said Shadow. "I can't wait to get my paws on that treasure chest. I bet it's filled with gold doubloons or precious jewels. We are going to be rich!"

"Maybe the treasure chest is filled with cheese," said Coco.

"*Cheese?*" scoffed Shadow.

"Sure," said Coco. "Grilled cheese or mac-and-cheese or just plain cheese. A whole treasure chest full of cheese. Yum."

"Whatever the treasure turns out to be," said Leopold, "we should hand it over to Mom and Dad. They'll know what to do with it."

"They should use it to buy a security system," whimpered Whiskers, "to protect us against pirate raids."

"Or," said Coco, "they could buy more cheese."

CHAPTER
7

Ring-ring!

Ring-ring!

Mom hurried into the Welcome Area from the office. Cassie followed her.

"Where did I leave that phone?" Mom said. She dug around the sofa cushions. "Whiskers, have you seen the phone?"

Ring-ring!

"Sounds like it's in the classroom," said Mom. She hurried off to find it.

"Hi, Coco," said Cassie, coming over and giving her a big hug. "It's almost time for lunch." Coco sighed happily.

Mom came back to the Welcome Area with the phone to her ear. "Sounds good. We'll see you Thursday for Fritz's grooming appointment. You'd like to use the e-mail coupon? Great."

Then she suddenly stopped.

"Wait . . . *fifty* percent off? Are you sure it doesn't say *five* percent off? Okay, then. We'll see you on Thursday."

Mom hung up the phone. "That's odd," she said. "I know I wrote 'five percent off.' And no one else has been on the computer today."

I looked at Leopold. Leopold looked at me.

Mom didn't know it, but someone else had been on her computer. *Two* someones to be exact.

"Is it time for lunch yet?" asked Cassie. "Look at poor Coco. She's so hungry."

"Tell you what," said Mom. "Let's take the dogs for a walk. We'll check on the guests in the barn and kennels. Then we'll come back and have a nice, relaxing lunch."

"Okay," said Cassie. She grabbed a leash and clipped it to Coco's collar.

Shadow rubbed against Cassie's leg. "Mom, can Shadow come too?"

Mom smiled. "Of course. Sometimes I think she's more dog than cat."

Cassie put on Shadow's leash. Yes, Shadow has a special cat leash.

As Mom attached my leash, she gave my head a pat. "I was hoping we could take a long walk in the woods today, Dash, but things are busier than—"

Ding-dong!

Mom opened the door. It was Martha, the groomer.

"Hi, guys," said Martha. She quickly shut the door. "It sure is getting blustery out there."

"Hi, Martha," said Mom. "Cassie and I are just heading over to the barn and kennels." Mom held up the phone. "Better bring this with us," she said, and laughed. "It's been ringing all morning."

Ding-dong!

"That must be Monsieur Petit," said Martha.

Monsieur Petit is a miniature French poodle. He's been coming to Animal Inn for his weekly

grooming appointment ever since we opened.

But it was not Monsieur Petit. It was a Labradoodle badly in need of a bath.

"What's that smell?" asked Cassie. The unmistakable aroma of skunk blew into the Welcome Area.

"Can we help you?" Mom said to the dog's owner.

"I hope so," said the woman. She wore a big, floppy hat, which she held on to with one hand, to keep it from blowing away. "I'm Wilhelmina, and this is Felix," she said, stepping inside and closing the door. "Felix is a bit . . . *skunky*. So when I received your coupon for fifty percent off, I thought, *Perfect!* And we came right over."

"*Fifty* percent off?" asked Martha.

"Small typo," Mom said sheepishly.

"I can take him after Monsieur Petit," Martha offered.

"Thank you," Mom said with a sigh. She turned to Felix's owner. "This is Martha, our groomer. Why don't I bring Felix to the outdoor play area until Martha's ready for him?"

Ding-dong!

"*That* must be Monsieur Petit," said Martha. She opened the door.

This time it *was* Monsieur Petit.

"Ooh la la," he muttered under his breath. "Something here is smellier than a French cheese."

"Mmm, cheese," moaned Coco.

"It's this guy," whispered Shadow, pointing with her crinkled nose.

"Sorry," mumbled Felix, a bit embarrassed.

Mom held Felix's leash in one hand and the phone in the other. "Cassie, do you have everybody else?"

Cassie nodded, gathering leashes.

"Okay, crew," said Mom. "Let's cast off!"

"I'll be back soon!" called Monsieur Petit's owner, Madame Gigi.

"I'll be back soon!" called Felix's owner, Wilhelmina.

I looked at Leopold. "I'll be back soon," I whispered.

CHAPTER
8

"Whoa!" shouted Cassie. "It's

windy out here!"

She was having a hard time holding on to the

leashes and keeping her hair out of her eyes.

"You walk ahead," Mom called to Cassie. "You

don't want to be downwind of Felix."

Poor Felix. He had probably just wanted to

play with the skunk but had gotten a little too

close. Now you could smell him a mile away.

"Let me put Felix in the play area," said Mom. "The fresh air will do him good."

Afterward she slid open the heavy barn door. The wind rushed in, blowing bits of hay into tiny cyclones.

We all piled inside. Mom slid the large door closed. Cassie undid all of our leashes. Shadow scampered straight to the loft. Coco flopped onto a mound of hay. I stayed close to Mom.

The building had once been a cow barn, but today our only guest was a beige-colored alpaca named Dandelion. She was staying with us while her owners repaired her shelter at home.

Mom raked out Dandelion's stall. She gave her fresh water. Cassie brought over some hay.

"Sorry I haven't gotten you out to the pasture

today," Mom said to Dandelion. "It's been busier than I expected."

"I think Dandelion's happy in here," said Cassie, gently stroking her neck. "It's too windy out there."

"She's right," Dandelion whispered to me with a toothy smile. We could all hear the wind blowing.

Coco and I followed Mom and Cassie to the back of the barn. Mom opened the door to the kennels. Each dog gets a private enclosure with a door to an outside run. On nice days the dogs are free to go in and out whenever they choose.

I always enjoy visiting the kennels and meeting new guests. Our current guests included a hound named Houdini, a Portuguese water dog named Walter, and a Pomeranian puppy named Penny.

The cats have smaller enclosures, each with

its own window to see outside.

We had only one feline guest, a cuddly calico named Cassandra.

I could hear Penny, the puppy, quietly crying in her kennel.

"What's wrong?" I asked her.

"Are you hungry?" asked Coco.

"I'm scared," Penny whimpered. "Too many strange noises."

The wind whistled. A tree branch cracked nearby. I was little scared too, and the pirates hadn't even arrived yet.

"It's just the wind," I said, trying to comfort her.

"I want to go home," Penny said.

Mom gave the dogs fresh water. Cassie refilled their food bowls. Then Mom noticed Penny cowering in the corner.

"Oh, little one," she said. "Not the best weather

for your first trip away from home."

Mom reached into Penny's kennel and picked

her up. "Why don't you come back to the inn

with us for a little bit?"

"Yay!" cheered Cassie. "Can I carry her?"

"Sure," said Mom.

Coco and I followed Mom and Cassie back into the barn.

"Shadow!" Cassie called. "It's time to go."

Ring-ring!

Ring-ring!

"Animal Inn," answered Mom.

Shadow appeared, her fur dotted with bits of hay. "Who's that in Cassie's arms?" she whispered to Coco and me.

"That's Penny," I said.

"She's a little nervous," said Coco.

"She should meet my brother," said Shadow.

Mom hung up the phone. "We'd better get back to the inn," she said to Cassie. "Our last-minute guests will be here momentarily. And I still don't know where to put that treasure."

CHAPTER
9

Back in the Welcome Area, Mom

and Cassie took off our leashes and hung them up.

"Let's find a comfy place for Penny on the third floor," Mom said to Cassie. "We can check on the upstairs guests, and then, I promise, we'll have lunch."

Cassie followed Mom upstairs, with Penny snuggled in her arms.

"Anything to report?" I asked Leopold.

"All quiet here," Leopold said. "Smooth sailing."

"Yes, very quiet," agreed Whiskers from the sofa. He stood up and stretched. "Monsieur Petit has already been picked up. Martha just brought Felix into the grooming room. He sure was stinky, but now I smell lavender. It's very relaxing. It might turn out to be a quiet day after all."

"Except—" I started.

"Except *what*?" Whiskers said with alarm.

"Except the pirates will be here any second," Shadow said with a grin.

"Why didn't anybody warn me?" asked Whiskers.

"We just found out ourselves," I said.

Whiskers gulped. "We need to do something."

"I'm too hungry to do anything," moaned Coco. "When's lunch?"

"Let's use the element of surprise," suggested Shadow. "When the pirates arrive, I'll leap out from behind the sofa and swipe at their ankles with a swish and a slash." Shadow made dramatic sword-fighting motions with her paws.

"Maybe I can speak with their parrot," said Leopold. "I always find talking to be the best strategy."

"I agree," I said. "We need to stay calm and—"

Whoosh!

The door blew open. The wind rushed in.

"Hit the deck!" cried Whiskers. "It's a raid!"

"It's just the wind," I said.

"Wait a minute," said Leopold. He flew over to the open door. Leaves and dust whipped and swirled outside. He slowly raised his head, trying to make out something in the distance.

"What are you looking at?" Whiskers asked nervously.

"It's hard to see, with the wind blowing leaves this way and that," Leopold said. "But I think there's a person coming up the driveway, walking strangely."

"Strangely?" asked Coco. "You mean like this?" Coco did a silly walk in front of the sofa.

"No," said Leopold. "The figure seems to be limping."

"Maybe it's a pirate with a peg leg," said Coco.

"There's only *one* pirate?" asked Shadow. "I can handle one pirate with my paws tied behind my back."

"Wait," said Leopold. "There are now two figures." He looked a little shaken.

"*Two* pirates?" shrieked Whiskers.

"The second one is carrying something heavy," added Leopold.

"I bet it's the treasure," said Shadow.

"Or a giant piece of cheese," said Coco.

"Hold on," said Leopold. He strained to see out the door. He held up a wing to protect his eyes from the wind. "I think I see a third figure."

"*Three* pirates?" squealed Whiskers. "Abandon ship!"

"Now, now," I said. "Let's steady ourselves."

"Or retreat," said Leopold. "The third one appears to have a sword."

CHAPTER
10

Whiskers let out an ear-piercing

yowl.

Shadow jumped behind the sofa.

Leopold retreated to his perch, and then raised one wing like a shield.

Coco pretended to be asleep.

I stood my ground, but I admit I closed my eyes. What would happen now? Would we have to walk the plank? Would we be buried with the treasure? Was this the end of Animal Inn?

The wind rushed in. I heard footsteps approaching. I slowly opened one eye. And there . . . in the doorway . . . stood . . .

Jake, Dad, and Ethan.

"Hi, guys," said Ethan.

"Why is the door open?" asked Dad.

Jake was standing on one leg, leaning on a walking stick. Dad carried a large duffel bag. Ethan held a tent pole like a sword.

Mom and Cassie rushed downstairs.

"What happened?" Mom asked, coming over to help them.

"Wind advisory," said Dad, shutting the door behind him. "We couldn't get the tent to stay up. Then Jake chased some napkins that went flying . . ."

"Tripped and twisted my ankle," Jake said with grimace.

"It was *so* windy," said Ethan, holding up the pole in his hand, "even the poles were blowing away."

"We could have used Coco and Dash," Dad said. "Lots of fetching to do. I think next time we'll find a campground that allows dogs."

Cassie smiled.

"Come on," said Mom. "We were just about to have lunch. I can whip up a few more grilled cheese sandwiches."

Coco stood up, bright-eyed and alert.

"Sounds great," said Dad. "We can unload the car later. I had to park down by the road. There's a fallen limb across the driveway."

"And let's get some ice on that ankle," Mom said to Jake.

They all went upstairs, Jake leaning on Dad and taking one stair at a time. Coco followed.

"I have to admit, I feel a little foolish," I said.

"Me too," said Leopold. "To think it was Dad and the boys the whole time."

"And not a band of pirates," said Whiskers. He laughed. "Leopold, you might want to get your eyes checked. Really? A peg leg and a sword?"

"Shhh!" whispered Shadow, popping out from behind the sofa. "Did you hear that?"

"Hear what?" asked Leopold.

Scritch-scritch!

Scritch-scritch!

"That!" said Shadow. She looked worried. And Shadow rarely looks worried.

"I think it's just the wind," I said.

"Now who's the scaredy-cat, Shadow?" said

Whiskers with a chuckle. He jumped down from the sofa and strutted over to the front door. "A few blustery pirates are no match for me."

Scritch-scritch!

Creeeeak!

The door opened a few inches. Leopold, Shadow, and I took a step back.

Whiskers bravely stood his ground. "It's just the wind," he said.

Whoooosh!

A sudden gust blew the door wide open. And there . . . in the doorway . . . we saw . . .

A tall figure wearing an eye-patch, with a parrot on its shoulder.

"Over here, Blackbeard!" the figure called. "This is the place!"

"*YOWWWL!*" Whiskers shrieked in fright. "*YOWWWL!*"

The pirate flinched. The parrot on its shoulder squawked in alarm, and then flew off into the gusty afternoon.

"Treasure!" shouted the figure, running after the bird. "Treasure! Come back!"

CHAPTER
11

"PI-RATE!" yelled Fuzzy, popping

out from the heating vent. He was completely out of breath.

"We spotted it from the crow's nest," added Furry, popping out next.

"You're a little late," said Shadow. "The pirate already abandoned ship. It took off after a parrot."

"I believe it was an African gray parrot," said Leopold.

"Whiskers scared it," said Shadow.

"I scared *it*?" Whiskers exclaimed. "It scared *me*."

"But where's the dog?" asked Fuzzy.

"What dog?" I asked.

"We definitely saw a pirate, a parrot, and a dog," added Furry.

Suddenly the pirate reappeared in the doorway. Whiskers's fur stood up on end. Fuzzy and Furry jumped back into the heating vent.

"Hello?" the pirate called into the Welcome Area. "Is anybody here? I need help!"

It didn't sound much like a pirate. It sounded more like a worried pet owner.

Mom and Dad rushed downstairs. Cassie and Coco followed.

"Can we help you?" asked Mom.

"I'm Annie," the woman said. "We spoke earlier.
But I just lost Treasure!"

"Oh no," gasped Mom. She turned to Dad.
"This is Annie Drake. Her pets are staying with us
while she has eye surgery."

Cassie looked around. "But where's Blackbeard?" she asked.

"He's already looking for Treasure," said Annie. "Treasure was in her harness, but then the wind blew and a cat yowled. Somehow she broke free and flew away."

"We should spread out and circle the area," said Dad.

"Cassie, you stay here," said Mom. "Tell the boys we'll be back soon."

Cassie headed upstairs. Mom, Dad, and Annie rushed outside. They were in such a hurry that no one checked to make sure the door was completely shut.

"Whew," said Whiskers. "I'm glad they're not real pirates. Now we can relax."

"Not quite," I said. "We need to help find Treasure."

"You mean outside?" cried Whiskers. "I'm an indoor cat."

"I'll stay here with Whiskers in case Treasure comes back," said Leopold.

"What about us?" said Fuzzy, popping back out of the heating vent.

"We know kung fu," added Furry.

"I don't think kung fu will be necessary," I said. "You two head back to the crow's nest and keep watch. Coco, you cover the yard. Shadow, you're in charge of bushes and hedges. I'll take the barn and kennels. We're going on a Treasure hunt!"

CHAPTER
12

I nudged the front door open

with my nose. The wind whipped and the leaves

swirled. We braced ourselves and headed outside.

Coco searched the yard. "Treasure," she called.

"Where are you, Treasure?"

Shadow searched in the hedges. "Treasure," I

heard her call. "Are you in here, Treasure?"

I hurried off to the barn and kennels. I could

see Mom, Dad, and Annie down by the road, still looking. But there was no sign of Treasure.

The barn door was open a little. Maybe Treasure had flown inside to escape the wind.

"Hi, Dash," said Dandelion, the alpaca. "Back so soon?"

"What?" I asked.

"Well, you just ran through, of course," said Dandelion.

I was confused. "Dandelion, have you seen a gray parrot?"

"Silly, you just asked me that!" said Dandelion with her toothy grin.

I scratched at the kennel door. It was shut tight.

"Can you hear me?" I called to the guests inside. "It's me, Dash. Has anyone seen a gray parrot?"

"No," Houdini, the hound, called back.

"But we'll keep an eye out," called Walter, the Portuguese water dog.

"Wait!" It was Cassandra, the calico cat. "Someone just flew by my window."

I ran back outside. But the only thing I saw flying by Cassandra's window was a huge leaf caught in the wind.

I scanned the field and sniffed at the air. Nothing.

I looked back toward Animal Inn. Nothing.

I looked down the driveway. Mom and Annie were standing next to Annie's car. I saw Mom put an arm around Annie's shoulders to comfort her.

Then I had a frightening thought.

What if we *didn't* find Treasure? It would be dark before long. Treasure would be outside in the wind and the cold. All alone.

Shiver me timbers. Maybe we were sunk.

Feeling defeated, I started toward to the inn. I hadn't taken more than a few steps when I felt something on my neck, clinging to my collar.

"Was that a lion that yowled?" said a small voice next to my ear. "Or a tiger?"

"Um—" I started.

"Whatever it was, it was scary," said the voice. "Right, Blackbeard?"

"Oh, my name's not—" I stopped talking. But I kept walking.

"I'm glad I found you, Blackbeard," said the voice. "I was so scared. And I don't want Annie to leave. And it's so windy today. And there was that lion noise. And my harness was loose. And then I got lost."

No doubt about it. I had found Treasure. Or rather, Treasure had found me.

She sighed. I could feel her body relax. I kept walking.

Then suddenly a dog came running across the field. It looked just like ... *me*! It was another Tibetan terrier. We were almost twins, except the fur on my chin is white, and the fur on its chin was black.

Now I understood. Black. Beard.

"Oh, hi, Blackbeard," said Treasure. Then I felt her suddenly stiffen. "Wait!" she said. "If you're Blackbeard ... who's *this*?"

Blackbeard smiled. "This is our lucky charm."

Treasure flew over to Blackbeard and looked back at me, a little confused.

"I'm Dash," I said. "Welcome to Animal Inn."

Blackbeard and I hit it off right away. Like I said, we Tibetan terriers make very good companions. Together we headed back to the inn. I could see

Fuzzy and Furry cheering from the crow's nest. Coco and Shadow met us at the front door.

Mom, Dad, and Annie came running up the driveway.

"Treasure!" said Annie. "My precious Treasure." She gently took Treasure from Blackbeard.

"Dash? Coco? Shadow?" Mom asked. "How did you three get out?"

"I guess all's well that ends well," said Dad.

We went inside to the Welcome Area. Whiskers was in his usual spot on the sofa. Leopold was on his perch. Jake, Ethan, and Cassie were downstairs too. Mom introduced everyone. Annie told the Tylers a little bit about herself and her pets.

"I'll be back in a few days to pick you up," Annie assured Blackbeard and Treasure. Mom and Dad walked Annie out to her car.

"Wow," said Jake. "Annie has the coolest job."

"I know," said Ethan.

"When I grow up," said Cassie, "I want to be a harbor pirate just like Annie."

"Cassie, it's harbor *pilot*. Not harbor *pirate*," corrected Ethan.

"That's what I said," insisted Cassie. "Harbor pirate." She tried hard to make the *L* sound, but it still came out like "pirate."

"Annie helps to guide ships, not raid and rob them," said Jake.

"Plus, why would a pirate ever come to Animal Inn?" said Ethan.

"Yeah, that would be ridiculous," said Cassie.

I looked at Leopold. Leopold looked at me.

Yes. Totally ridiculous.

EPILOGUE

I learned a lot of important

lessons from our pirate scare:

1. Wearing an eye-patch and owning a parrot do not necessarily make you a pirate.

2. Treasures come in all shapes and sizes.

3. A fifty-percent-off coupon can be very good for business.

4. Sooner or later crows will come back to

roost. (And they don't mind gerbils so much.)

By Sunday morning Animal Inn was like a calm sea. The sky was blue. The wind had disappeared. It was a perfect day.

Mom took Blackbeard and me on a long walk in the woods.

Jake's ankle felt better after he had a good night's sleep.

Ethan told Leopold all about the camping adventure.

And Cassie found the perfect place to keep Annie's Treasure—*in her room*.

"Penny, Treasure, and I slept very well last night," said Cassie.

"But I put Penny on the third floor," said Mom.

"Well . . . ," said Cassie with a smile.

Dad came in from clearing the tree limb that had been blocking the driveway.

"I might need glasses," he said.

"Why?" asked Mom.

"I'm positive I just saw Fuzzy and Furry on the roof," said Dad, scratching his head. "It looked like they were having a conversation with some crows."

"That's impossible," said Ethan.

"They're in the gerbiltorium," said Jake.

"Are you sure?" asked Mom.

Ethan rushed upstairs to check. Jake limped close behind.

Ding-dong!

"That's probably another customer with a coupon," said Mom, sighing.

"You relax," said Dad. "I'll get it."

 **194**

But it wasn't a customer. It was a delivery person.

"Special delivery," she said.

Dad took the package and thanked her. He turned to Mom, a bit puzzled. "I didn't order anything. Did you?"

"Not me," said Mom. "Who's it from?"

Dad looked at the mailing label. "Picture *Purr*fect?" he said.

"Can I open it?" begged Cassie. *"Please."*

Cassie opened the box. Packing peanuts tumbled onto the floor.

"It's a photo!" said Cassie. She held it up for Mom and Dad to see. "It's so cute."

Mom and Dad sure looked confused.

"I didn't order it," said Mom.

"Me either," said Dad.

"We can hang it in the office," Cassie said excitedly.

"I guess I'll get the hammer," said Dad.

"I'll get a picture hook," said Mom. "But who would send us a framed photo of Fuzzy and Furry?"

I looked at Leopold. Leopold looked at me.

Those little scallywags.

The Bow-wow Bus

For Annie W.

PROLOGUE

Beep-beep!

Beep-beep!

Yippee! The school bus is here.

Beep-beep!

Welcome to Animal Inn. My name is Coco. I'm a chocolate Labrador retriever.

No, I'm not made of chocolate, silly. I don't even like the stuff. We dogs aren't supposed to eat chocolate. But I do like to eat. Especially cheese.

I like cheddar cheese and Swiss cheese and American cheese.

I like cheese sticks and cheese balls and cheese puffs.

I like mac-and-cheese and grilled cheese and cheese pizza.

Luckily, my human sister, Cassie, likes cheese as much as I do. Cassie and I belong to the Tyler family. Our family includes five humans—Mom, Dad, Jake, Ethan, and Cassie—and seven pets:

- Me
- Dash—a Tibetan terrier
- Leopold—a scarlet macaw
- Shadow and Whiskers—sister and brother cats
- and Fuzzy and Furry—a pair of very adventurous gerbils

The Tylers used to live in an apartment in the city. Back then, Mom and Dad had two children, Jake and Ethan, and two pets, Dash and Leopold. But when Cassie and I came along, Mom and Dad bought this old house in the country.

Animal Inn is one part hotel, one part school, and one part spa. As our brochure says, *We promise to love your pet as much as you do.*

Beep-beep!

Where are Jake, Ethan, and Cassie? It's time for them to go to school.

Before long, customers will start to arrive. On some days, there is so much coming and going, Animal Inn could use a revolving door. We might have a Pekinese here for a pedicure. A Siamese for a short stay. Or a llama for a long stay.

On the first floor, we have the Welcome Area,

the office, the classroom, the grooming room, and my favorite—the party and play room.

Our family lives on the second floor. This includes Fuzzy and Furry snug in their gerbiltorium in Jake and Ethan's room.

The third floor is for smaller guests. We have a Reptile Room, a Rodent Room, and a Small Mammal Room. Larger guests stay out in the barn and kennels.

Beep-beep!

Where are those kids?

What if they miss the bus? What if they miss school?

School is so awesome. There's story time and lunchtime and playtime. In fact, just last week I got to spend an entire day with Cassie's first-grade class. Let me tell you what happened. . . .

CHAPTER 1

It began like any other Monday.

When Cassie and I came downstairs that morning, Leopold was already on his perch. Dash sat nearby. Whiskers was curled up on the sofa, while Shadow hid behind it. (She likes to sneak outside whenever she gets the chance.)

Cassie was chattering to me as usual. "My school job this week is snack helper," she said. She unzipped her backpack and pulled out her lunch box. "Sit please, Princess Coco."

I sat. Cassie opened her lunch box and took out a little snack-pack filled with cubes of cheese. She gave one to me.

Yum. Cheddar.

"Now, if you have a question," Cassie said to me, "you need to raise your paw." She held up another piece of cheese. "Show me your paw, please."

I raised my paw.

"Very good, Princess Coco. But I won't be able to call you 'Princess,'" she said sadly. "In first grade, make-believe is only for recess and choice time. So in class, I will just call you Coco."

Cassie backed up a few steps and patted her thighs. "Come, Coco," she called.

I trotted over and nudged her hand with my

nose. She gave me another piece of cheese.

"Now for the fun part," Cassie said. She went to the supply closet and found her old backpack from preschool—the one that looks like a ladybug. I'd worn Cassie's ladybug backpack before, like the time we ran away to the barn.

Dash looked at Leopold. Leopold looked at Dash. Whiskers looked a little nervous. But I was curious. What was Cassie up to now?

"Sit please, Princess Coco. I mean, just Coco."

I sat.

"Show me your paw, Coco."

I raised a paw. Cassie held it in her hand. She gently guided my paw through the shoulder strap of the backpack. Then she guided my other paw through the other strap. The backpack was a little wobbly, so Cassie tightened it up.

"Cassie!" Mom called from upstairs. "Did you remember to brush your teeth?"

"Oops," Cassie said. "I'll be right back," she whispered to me. "You stay here." She tossed me another cube of cheese. She put the snack-pack back into her lunch box and set it next to the sofa. Then she ran up the stairs.

I plopped down on the floor. Whew! That was a lot of activity for so early in the morning.

Shadow came out from her hiding spot behind the sofa. "What's with the ladybug?" she asked me. "Are you and Cassie running away again?"

"Don't be silly," I said. "It's a school day."

"Then why are you wearing a backpack?" asked Whiskers.

"Cassie put it there," I said.

"We know that," said Shadow. "But *why*?"

"It appears Cassie is bringing Coco to school today," said Dash.

"I agree," said Leopold. "Weekly job assignment. Question protocol. Make-believe-play rules."

"Well, I'm glad *I'm* not the one going to school," said Whiskers.

"I am not going to school," I said. I stretched out in my sunny spot. "I am going to take a nap."

CHAPTER
2

Jake, Ethan, and Cassie ran

downstairs.

"Cassie, why is Coco wearing your ladybug backpack?" Jake asked.

"Are you running away to the barn again?" said Ethan.

"No, silly," answered Cassie. "It's a school day."

"Boys!" Dad called from upstairs. "Did you remember to feed Fuzzy and Furry?"

"Ethan fed them," Jake answered.

"I didn't feed them," said Ethan. "I thought you fed them."

"It's your turn," said Jake.

"I thought it was your turn," said Ethan.

The boys dropped their backpacks and ran upstairs, almost bumping into Mom and Dad, who were on their way down.

"Cassie," said Mom, "are you all set for show-and-tell today?"

Cassie nodded. She unzipped her backpack and pulled out a dog show ribbon. "I'm going to show this," she said.

The ribbon was purple and shiny. In fancy gold letters, it said *1st Place.*

Cassie came over to me and held the ribbon to
my collar.

"Coco is going to be my show dog," she said. "I
am going to *show* her for show-and-tell."

"But, sweetheart," said Dad, "you can't bring
Coco to school."

"I'm afraid Dad is right," said Mom. "Coco has to stay home today."

"But I told everyone they would get to meet Coco," said Cassie. "I told Helena and Mattias and Lucy and Seiji and Arlen and Laura." She reluctantly took off my ladybug backpack.

I didn't like to see Cassie sad. I nuzzled her with my nose. I wanted her to know that I was just fine staying home.

"I have an idea," said Dad. He leaned down and whispered something into Cassie's ear. Cassie's sad face suddenly turned into a happy face.

"I can't believe it!" Cassie squealed excitedly. "Do you really think so?"

"It can't hurt to ask," said Dad. "I'll call the school this morning."

Beep-beep!

Beep-beep!

"Jake! Ethan!" Mom called upstairs. "The bus is here."

The boys hurried down, picked up their backpacks, and rushed out the front door. Cassie gave me a big hug and stuffed the ribbon into her backpack. Then she skipped out the door after the boys. Mom and Dad followed.

"I can't believe it!" I heard Cassie squeal again. "Now my whole class will get to meet *all* my pets!"

CHAPTER

3

"What did Cassie just say?"
Whiskers asked with concern.

"I believe she said, *Now my whole class will get to meet all my pets,*" said Leopold. He even sounded like Cassie. Leopold is very good at repeating things.

"We're *all* going to school?" said Whiskers. "I just want to stay on my sofa."

"Let's not get ahead of ourselves," said Dash.

"We can't believe everything we hear from Cassie. Remember what happened with Miss KD?"

Miss KD was a Komodo dragon who bunked in our basement. There were a lot of misunderstandings before she arrived. We overheard Cassie say a wizard was coming to Animal Inn. But the "wizard" turned out to be a *lizard*.

"And let's not forget the incident with the pirate," said Leopold.

Not long ago, we overheard Cassie say a harbor pirate was coming to Animal Inn. But the harbor "pirate" turned out to be a harbor *pilot* named Annie. It didn't help that Annie's dog was called Blackbeard, just like the famous buccaneer.

"But you heard her," said Whiskers. "Cassie said her whole class will get to meet all her pets. Right, Shadow?"

Shadow didn't answer. Where was she?

"Excuse me," said a tiny voice. "I used to be in a school."

It was Blub.

Blub is a goldfish who was dropped off at Animal Inn a few weeks ago. Blub's owner went on a short business trip that turned into a long business trip that turned into an even longer business trip. In the meantime, Blub stayed in a fishbowl in the Welcome Area. It was just temporary, until his owner came back for him.

"I liked my school," continued Blub. "Fresh Pond Elementary. I had lots of friends. There was Goldie and Bubbles and Finn. I was even on the swim team." Blub swam a quick lap around his bowl.

I was about to ask Blub more about his school, when Mom and Dad came back from walking

the kids to the bus stop. They both seemed very excited.

"I'll call Cassie's teacher, Mr. C., right now," said Dad.

"I think this is a great idea," said Mom. She and Dad made their way to the office.

Dash looked at Leopold. Leopold looked at Dash.

Maybe we were going to school after all. But before I could give it another thought, I noticed the scent of cheese. I followed it to . . . Cassie's lunch box?

"Not again," I said. I picked up the lunch box in my mouth. The handle didn't taste very good.

Ding-dong!

Mom hurried out of the office. "What've you got there, Coco?" she asked. "Oh no. Did Cassie forget her lunch again?"

Mom took the lunch box from me and patted my head. Then she opened the front door. It was Sierra, our college intern.

"Good morning," said Mom.

"Good morning," said Sierra. "Look who I found outside." Sierra had her bike helmet under one arm and Shadow under the other.

"Shadow, you little sneak," said Mom.

Shadow skittered back behind the sofa.

I walked over to Sierra and sniffed her bag.

"Coco," Mom said with a laugh, "that's not polite."

"It's okay," said Sierra. "She knows I have treats in here." Sierra always brings us treats, like Doggie Donuts and Kitty Krisps. Yum.

I sat down at Sierra's feet and wagged my tail. She reached into her bag and pulled out a Doggie Donut. She tossed it in the air.

I caught it. It was cheese-and-bacon-flavored!
Double yum.

"How's my favorite sofa-surfer?" Sierra asked
Whiskers. She placed a Kitty Krisp next to him.
Whiskers actually started purring.

Sierra tossed another Kitty Krisp behind the

sofa for Shadow. She gave a Doggie Donut to Dash and a seed pop to Leopold.

"And . . . ," Sierra said with a smile. She reached deeper into her bag. "I even remembered a treat for Blub today." She walked over and sprinkled a handful of colorful flakes into Blub's bowl.

Sierra touched her fingertip to the surface of the water. Blub gently bumped it with his nose. "Goldfish high-five!" she cheered. "Any word from Blub's owner?" she asked Mom.

"Just got an e-mail," said Mom. "It looks like Blub might be with us for a while yet."

"Well, what's the plan for this morning?" asked Sierra.

"The Rodent Room and Small Mammal Room need some attention," said Mom.

"Hi, Sierra," said Dad, coming out of the office.

"Did you reach Mr. C.?" Mom asked Dad.

"Yes, great news. He loves the idea."

We animals perked up our ears.

"What idea?" asked Sierra.

"The pets are going to visit with Cassie's class," said Mom. "Do you think you might be able to help out?"

"It shouldn't be a problem," said Sierra. "When's the visit?"

"That's the best part," Dad said excitedly. He started following Mom and Sierra up the stairs. "It's *tomorrow*!"

CHAPTER 4

"**Tomorrow?**" **Whiskers said** nervously.

Shadow emerged from behind the sofa, still chomping on her treat. "What's going on tomorrow?" she asked, her mouth full of crumbs.

"It appears we are all going to school," said Leopold.

"Sounds cool," said Shadow. "What are we doing there?"

"Not sure," said Dash. "But I know how we can find out. Follow me to the gerbiltorium."

We all hurried upstairs to Jake and Ethan's room. Fuzzy and Furry were lounging in one of their play structures.

"Greetings, friends," said Fuzzy.

"Care for a snack?" added Furry. He was nibbling on a cashew.

"No thanks," said Dash. "We've got a job for you and we need to hurry."

"Speed is our specialty," said Fuzzy.

"But it's an additional charge," added Furry.

"I believe after what happened last time," said Leopold, "this job should be for free."

For their last job, Fuzzy and Furry were supposed to print an e-mail from the computer in the office. Instead, they ordered a framed photo of themselves. Mom and Dad are still trying to figure out where it came from.

"Point taken," said Fuzzy.

"Give us the lowdown," added Furry.

"Lucky for us, Cassie forgot her lunch box again," said Dash. "Mom or Dad will have to bring it to school, and you two are going to hide inside it."

"When you get to Cassie's classroom," Leopold added, "sneak out and investigate."

"We need all the information you can find about pets going to school," said Dash.

"You got it," said Fuzzy. "Except . . ."

"Except what?" asked Shadow.

"The plan will never work," added Furry.

"Why not?" asked Dash.

"How do we get home?" asked Fuzzy.

"We're not exactly flying squirrels," added Furry.

"I hadn't thought about that," said Dash. He looked at Leopold. Leopold shrugged.

"I have an idea," I said.

"I can't wait to hear this," said Shadow. "Does it involve cheese?"

"No, silly," I said. "What if Fuzzy and Furry stay at school for the whole day? Then they can sneak back into Cassie's lunch box and take the school bus home with the kids."

"That's quite brilliant," said Leopold.

"They'll have plenty of time," said Dash.

"Are we sure these two rodents can handle school?" asked Shadow.

"See this?" said Fuzzy, holding up a cashew.

"Brain food," added Furry.

They giggled and picked the lock on the gerbil-torium. Then they scurried into the heating vent and disappeared.

CHAPTER

5

By the time we got back to the

Welcome Area, Fuzzy and Furry were already

inside the lunch box. It wiggled ever so slightly.

Dad came down from the third floor. "I'm tak-

ing Cassie's lunch box to school," he called upstairs.

"Be right back."

Dad picked up the lunch box. "Sure feels like a

big lunch," he said on his way out the door. If he only knew.

I stretched out in my sunny spot. There was nothing to do now but wait. "I hope Cassie didn't miss lunchtime," I said.

"Lunchtime is usually at noon," said Whiskers matter-of-factly. "Recess is generally right after lunch. Then dismissal is at about three o'clock."

"How do you know so much about school?" I asked.

"Don't you remember, Coco?" said Shadow. "Whiskers and I lived in a schoolyard when we were kittens."

"I didn't like it," said Whiskers. "One time, there was a fire drill. The alarm was so loud."

"Come on, Little Brother," said Shadow. "It

wasn't that bad. We had a place to sleep under the play structure and all the cafeteria leftovers we could eat."

"But it was cold in the winter," said Whiskers. "And we didn't have a family."

I still remember the day Shadow and Whiskers arrived at Animal Inn. I was just a pup then. We hadn't been open very long when a nice man named Mr. Raymond showed up at the front door with a cardboard box. Shadow and Whiskers were inside. They were so cute.

"Well, it all turned out for the best," I said.

"I still didn't like it," said Whiskers.

"I liked my school," said Blub, in his tiny voice. "We played lots of games, like Fishy, Fishy, Cross My Ocean and Go Fish!" Blub sighed. Small bubbles floated to the top of his bowl.

"I liked my school too," said Dash. "When I was young, I went to a show dog academy. We learned lots of important skills."

"What about you, Leopold?" I asked. "Have you ever been to school?"

"I'm what you might call homeschooled," said Leopold. "I've learned everything I know right here."

"Me too!" I said. "I learned how to read in the Furry Pages. I started with beginner books, like *Go, Dog. Go!* But now I can read chapter books, like Henry and Mudge, with a little help."

Every Saturday, Dad and Jake host a class called the Furry Pages, where children read aloud to an animal buddy. I love the Furry Pages. If Cassie's class was anything like that, we had nothing to worry about.

"I think school will be fun," I said.

Ding-dong!

Mom came downstairs to open the door. It was Martha, the Animal Inn groomer.

"Good morning, everybody," said Martha.

"Hi, Martha," said Mom. "Listen, we need to add a few customers to your schedule today. The Tyler pets all need a brush and a trim."

"No problem," said Martha. "What's the occasion?"

"School visit," said Mom, heading for the stairs.

"Sounds exciting," said Martha.

Ding-dong!

"I'll get it," called Martha. She opened the front door. It was our good friend Sheila the shar-pei, here for a shampoo.

"Hello, cuddly Coco," Sheila whispered as she passed by. "Nice to see you, wonderful Whiskers.

Good morning, darling Dash. Greetings, lovely Leopold. What's new, shimmering Shadow? Hi there, beautiful Blub."

Sheila followed Martha into the grooming room.

"Get ready, Whiskers," Martha called back to the Welcome Area. "You're next!"

CHAPTER
6

"Who knew hamsters could make

such a mess?" said Mom, coming down the stairs.

She wiped her arm across her brow.

"They do like to hide food in funny places,"

said Sierra.

Ding-dong!

Mom answered the door.

"Hello," said a man. "I'm Andrew Patel, and this

is my new dog, Lucky. He'll be staying with you for a few days."

"Yes, we're expecting you," said Mom. "Welcome to Animal Inn."

Lucky was a medium-size hound dog. I love meeting new friends. I walked over to say hello.

Woof-woof-woof-woof-woof!

Lucky barked and barked.

"I'm afraid Lucky's not that good with other dogs," Mr. Patel said over the loud barking. "He's a rescue pup."

Woof-woof-woof-woof-woof!

"Maybe a treat would help," said Sierra. She slowly walked over to Lucky. Then she bent down and offered him a Doggie Donut. "Here you go, my friend," she said calmly.

Lucky took the treat.

"It's yummy, right?" I whispered to him.

Lucky nodded and lay down at Sierra's feet, chewing happily.

"That's amazing," said Mr. Patel. "Lucky can get a little nervous, but he calmed right down with you. You're so good with him."

"Yes, Sierra is our incredible intern," said Mom. "Why don't you go ahead and give Lucky to her. She can get him settled in his kennel."

"I'll bring Coco, too," said Sierra. She grabbed my leash from the hook by the door. "Looks like Lucky could use a friend."

"Bye, Lucky," said Mr. Patel, reaching down to pat his head. "Be a good dog. I'll be back for you soon. It's only for a few days."

Sierra, Lucky, and I headed outside. It felt good to get a little fresh air.

"I'm Coco," I whispered to Lucky. "Welcome to Animal Inn. You'll like it here. We promise to love you as much as your owner does."

"Which one?" Lucky asked.

"What do you mean?" I said.

"Which owner?" said Lucky. "My first owner moved to a new apartment and couldn't have a dog. He gave me back to the shelter. My second owner didn't have time for a puppy. So she gave me back to the shelter. My third owner turned out to be allergic to dogs. He gave me back to the shelter. Mr. Patel is my fourth owner. Lucky is my fourth name. And now Mr. Patel's leaving me here," he said sadly.

"It's only for a few days," I offered.

"That's what my last owner told me." Lucky said.

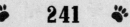 **241**

Sierra slid open the barn door. Today our only barn guest was an Angora goat named Toni. She was so fluffy.

"Hi, Toni," I said as we passed by. "This is Lucky."

"Pleased to meet you, Lucky," said Toni.

Sierra walked us to the back of the barn and opened the door to the kennels. She got Lucky settled in his enclosure and gave him a whole handful of Doggie Donuts. She filled his water bowl and fluffed up the dog bed in the corner. Then she opened the door to his outside run.

"Your owner will be back for you soon," I whispered to Lucky. "I'm sure of it."

CHAPTER
7

When we got back to the Welcome

Area, Sierra hung up my leash. Then she went to find Mom.

Sheila the shar-pei was just leaving. She looked very stylish.

"Toodle-loo, cuddly Coco," Sheila whispered as she followed Martha to the door. "Always a pleasure, wonderful Whiskers. See you, darling

Dash. So long, lovely Leopold. Are you back there, shimmering Shadow? Bye-bye, beautiful Blub."

"You're next, my dear," Martha said to Whiskers. She gently picked him up off the sofa and carried him back to the grooming room. Whiskers did not look happy.

"How's Lucky doing?" asked Dash.

"Okay," I said. "Did you know that he's had *four* families? His owners keep giving him away."

"Poor chap," said Leopold.

"I'm just happy we don't have to worry about that," I said. I settled down on the floor and closed my eyes. Even dogs like catnaps.

When Martha brought Whiskers out a little while later, his coat was brushed and very shiny.

"You look handsome," I whispered to Whiskers.

 **245**

"I need to clean up the room a bit," Martha said. "Then it's your turn, Shadow."

"Humph," I heard from behind the sofa.

Just then, the front door opened. Dad was back. "I'm home," he said.

"How did it go?" Mom called from the party and play room.

"Great," said Dad, going to join Mom. "Everyone will be included."

Included in what? I wondered. I sure hoped Fuzzy and Furry came back with some answers.

Suddenly, we heard a loud voice. "Can I please have your attention? Would Dash Tyler, Leopold Tyler, Coco Tyler, Shadow Tyler, and Whiskers Tyler report to the principal's office."

"Immediately!" said another voice.

We all froze. Even Dash and Leopold looked a little nervous.

Then we heard a giggle. And another giggle. Fuzzy popped out of the heating vent with a grin. Furry followed close behind.

"Did we get your attention?" asked Fuzzy.

"Just a little something we heard at school," added Furry.

"I thought the plan was for you to take the bus home," I said.

"Dad ended up chatting with Cassie's teacher for a while," said Fuzzy.

"We had plenty of time," added Furry.

"What did you find out?" asked Dash.

"Brace yourselves," said Fuzzy.

"Stay strong," added Furry.

"The entire school . . . ," said Fuzzy.

"Is nut free!" added Furry.

"Well, there were a least two nuts there," snickered Shadow.

"And we saw a poster," said Fuzzy.

"For a gigantic spelling bee," added Furry.

"Imagine," said Fuzzy. "A gigantic bee."

"That can *spell*!" added Furry.

"My dear friends," said Leopold, "a spelling bee is a competition, not an insect."

"That's right," said Dash. "It's nothing to worry about."

"Then worry about this!" said Fuzzy. "We heard Denise, the school nurse, talking. One of the kids has a bug. . . ."

"In her tummy!" added Furry.

"Guys, focus," said Dash. "What about Cassie's

classroom? Did you find anything there?"

"They have an aquarium," said Fuzzy.

"It is very soothing," added Furry.

"None of this information is very helpful," said Shadow.

"I have to agree," said Leopold. "Was there anything else?"

"Yes," said Fuzzy. "We saw Cassie's teacher throw this into the recycling bin." Fuzzy pulled a small square of folded paper out of the heating vent.

"It's part of a note," added Furry, "going home in folders today."

"I can read it," I said.

Fuzzy and Furry worked together to unfold the strip of paper. Then they ran back and forth to smooth it out.

"'Dear First-Grade Families,'" I read aloud.

"'Please join us tomorrow (yes, TOMORROW!) as we meet the pets of Animal Inn. We will be...'"

"We will be . . . We will be . . . what?" asked Whiskers.

"That's all it says," I told him. "The page is torn."

"Figures," said Shadow. "I knew I should have gone with them."

"What now?" I asked.

Dash looked at Leopold. Leopold looked at Dash. "We're not sure," they both said at the same time.

"Well, I plan to be absent," grumbled Whiskers.

"But being part of a school is fun," said a tiny voice. It was Blub again.

I padded over to his bowl. "Do you think you can join us tomorrow, Blub?" I asked.

"I'd better stay here in case my owner comes to pick me up," he gurgled.

"He'll be back for you soon," I whispered.

I had just said the same thing to Lucky. I sure hoped I was right.

CHAPTER
8

"Shadow," called Martha, **"it's** your turn."

Shadow darted behind the sofa.

"Look what Sierra gave me," said Martha. "Your favorite." Martha sprinkled a line of Kitty Krisps on the floor.

"Too . . . yummy . . . to . . . resist," Shadow whis-

pered between mouthfuls. Martha quickly scooped

her up.

"Drat," Shadow muttered as she was carried

away.

When Shadow returned a little while later,

she wore a new collar with a tinkling bell. "Now everybody will know where I am," she huffed under her breath.

"Coco, your turn," said Martha. "Dash is on deck. And last, but certainly not least, will be Leopold."

Martha gave me the works—bath, brush, and blow dry. I love the smell of Martha's shampoos.

When I was finished, Martha walked me back to the Welcome Area. I found a sunny spot and settled down for an afternoon nap. I soon fell into the strangest dream.

All the pets were there. I was driving the bus to school, but I didn't know which way to go. Fuzzy and Furry said they could help with directions. They would be my GPS—Gerbil Positioning System.

Whiskers kept telling me to slow down, but Shadow kept telling me to go faster. Dash and Leopold were leaning out the open window, enjoying the wind in their fur and feathers. Driving the bus was so cool! *Vroom! Vroom! Vroom!*

"Wake up, Princess Coco," Cassie said in a soft voice. "Wake up."

I slowly opened my eyes. I saw Mom and Dad and Jake and Ethan and Cassie. The kids were home from school! I wagged my tail.

"Hi, Dash," said Jake.

"Hi, Leopold," said Ethan. "You guys look nice."

"Shadow and Whiskers look great too," said Jake.

"I love Shadow's new bell!" cheered Cassie.

"Everyone is spiffed up and ready for the visit tomorrow," said Mom.

"And listen to this," Dad said. "Mr. C. and I had an idea. Animal Inn is going to donate a pet to the class."

"What does 'donate' mean?" asked Cassie.

I was glad she asked, because I didn't know either. I was hoping "donate" had something to do with "donuts."

"It means to give," said Ethan.

"More specifically, it means to give *away*," said Jake. "Like a present."

What? Give away a pet?

"I think it's a great idea," said Mom.

She did?

"And I know just the pet," said Dad.

He did? Was I still dreaming?

"My school friends are going to love my animal friends," said Cassie. "Shadow, you are going to love Lucy. She might even scoop you up and take you home with her."

What? Was Cassie going to let Lucy take Shadow?

Cassie skipped over to Dash. "Dash, you and Helena are both very helpful. And Helena always wanted a dog."

Was Cassie going to give Dash to Helena?

"Leopold, you are going to love Mattias," continued Cassie. "Mattias won the first-grade spelling bee."

So it *was* a spelling bee and not a bumblebee. At least *that* was good news.

But how could the Tylers give Leopold away?

"Whiskers, you and Seiji are going to be fast friends," Cassie said. "Seiji gets a little nervous too. He'll take good care of you."

Was Seiji going to take Whiskers?

Then Cassie skipped over to me. "And Mr. C. will just love you, Coco. He loves anything chocolate. He might just eat you up."

Gulp!

"Who's ready for a snack?" asked Mom.

Jake, Ethan, and Cassie raced upstairs. Mom and Dad followed.

Usually, I followed too. Cassie always shared her afterschool snack with me. But this time, I stayed just where I was.

I had lost my appetite.

"Are they really giving one of

us to Cassie's class?" I asked.

"Donating," said Leopold.

"It's the same thing," Whiskers insisted.

"Let's slow down," said Dash. "What exactly did

Dad say?"

"I'm afraid I heard the same as Coco," said

Leopold. "Animal Inn will donate a pet to Cassie's class."

"And Dad knows just the pet," I said sadly.

"Who do you think it is?" asked Whiskers.

"Well, we know it's not Dash," said Shadow. "Dash is a dog-show champion. And Mom's had him for, like, a million years."

"I'm not that old," said Dash.

"I doubt it could be me," said Leopold, nervously preening his feathers. "I believe a macaw is too sophisticated a pet for your average first grader."

"Well, it can't be me," said Shadow. "You can't have an outdoor cat as a classroom pet."

"But I'm an indoor cat," Whiskers whimpered.

"Calm down, Little Brother," said Shadow. "Mom and Dad would never separate us."

If it wasn't Dash or Leopold or Shadow or Whiskers, that left . . . me.

Just then, Fuzzy and Furry popped out of the heating vent.

"We hear Shadow has a new collar," said Fuzzy.

"We can literally hear it," added Furry.

"Very funny," said Shadow. She tried to shake the collar loose, but it only made the little bell ring more. "Drat," she muttered.

"Could it be Fuzzy or Furry?" Whiskers asked.

"Could what be Fuzzy?" asked Fuzzy.

"Or Furry?" added Furry.

"Mom and Dad are giving one of us away to Cassie's class," I said.

"But we're Jake and Ethan's pets," said Fuzzy.

"We're not Mom and Dad's to give," added Furry.

"Well, it's not going to be me!" cried Whiskers.

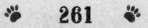

"What are we going to do?" I asked. I didn't care how much Mr. C. loved chocolate things. I didn't want to be given away. I didn't want a new family.

"Maybe they meant temporarily," said Fuzzy.

"Like only for a few days," added Furry.

Gulp!

That's exactly what Lucky's last owner had said.

CHAPTER
10

That night, I couldn't sleep.

Usually I feel safe and cozy, snuggled at the foot of Cassie's bed. Instead, I tossed and turned. Would the Tylers really give one of us away?

I could hear Leopold in his sleeping cage in the corner of the room. He was talking in his sleep. It sounded like he was having a bad dream.

I wondered about Dash at the foot of Jake's

bed, and Shadow and Whiskers in Mom and Dad's rocking chair. Were they as worried and confused as I was?

When I came downstairs the next morning, the other pets were already in the Welcome Area. It didn't look like anyone had slept well.

Cassie, on the other hand, seemed to have slept just fine. But something was odd. She didn't have her backpack and she was still in her pajamas, the footie ones covered in dancing lambs.

"I can't believe it, Princess Coco!" Cassie sang. She skipped over to me and tickled me behind the ears. Then she bounced over to the sofa and plopped down next to Whiskers.

"I just can't believe it!" Cassie sang again. She held Whiskers's front paws and did a little dance. Whiskers did not look happy.

"Leopold," Cassie said with a smile, "can you believe it?"

"Leopold cannot believe it," Leopold squawked from his perch. Cassie had taught him that.

"This is going to be the best day ever!" cheered Cassie, giving Dash a hug.

"Cassie!" Mom called from upstairs. "You still need to brush your teeth, even if you're not going to school."

"Coming!" sang Cassie. She ran back up the stairs.

"Cassie's not going to school today?" Whiskers asked.

"I hope not," said Shadow, stepping out from behind the sofa. "Not in those lambie jammies."

"At this rate, she'll never make it to the bus on time," said Leopold.

Just then, Jake and Ethan came downstairs. Mom and Dad followed. Mom was carrying a big cardboard box. It looked heavy.

"Ethan, did you feed Fuzzy and Furry?" asked Jake.

"Uh, yeah," said Ethan. "I did."

"Oh," said Jake, a bit surprised. "Good."

"I'll walk you to the bus stop," said Dad. "I'm heading out to do the morning chores in the barn and kennels."

"Please give Lucky a little extra attention," said Mom, trying to balance the box in her arms. "He still seems a bit gloomy."

"Will do," said Dad.

Beep-beep!

Beep-beep!

"You better hurry, boys," said Mom. "Have a great day." Then she carried the box to the party and play room.

"Cassie must be staying home sick today," said Whiskers. "I couldn't be happier."

"You're happy that Cassie is sick?" I asked.

"I'm not happy that she's sick," Whiskers

explained. "I'm happy that she's not going to school."

"Cassie does not appear to be sick," said Leopold.

"When Cassie's sick, we stay in bed and listen to an audiobook," I said. "Mom gives us warm milk and crackers."

"I know," Shadow piped up. "It's a teacher meeting day. Those teachers are always having meetings."

"Then why did Jake and Ethan go to school?" Dash asked.

"They all attend the same school," said Leopold.

"All that matters," said Whiskers, "is that Cassie is not going to school. That means *we* are not going to school. That means I can stay right here in peace." He snuggled down into the sofa cushions.

I thought for a moment. "If no pets are going to school," I said, "then no pets can be given away to the class."

I took a deep breath. Everything was back to normal.

At least, I hoped.

CHAPTER
11

Beep-beep!

Beep-beep!

"Yippee!" cheered Cassie. "The bus is here!"

Cassie had changed out of her jammies and was now wearing her Animal Inn T-shirt and a pair of jeans. She ran out the front door. Mom and Dad followed close behind.

"Why is the bus back?" Whiskers asked nervously.

"This is highly unusual," said Leopold.

Fuzzy and Furry skittered out of the heating vent.

"There's a big yellow bus outside!" announced Fuzzy.

"We spied it from the crow's nest," added Furry.

"You're a little late," said Shadow, slinking out from behind the sofa.

"Well, there's a lot of them," said Fuzzy.

"I counted twenty-five," added Furry.

"Twenty-five!" cried Whiskers

"Twenty-five what?" asked Dash.

Before the gerbils could answer, the front door swung open.

Fuzzy and Furry disappeared into the heating vent. Whiskers buried his head under a cushion. Shadow scampered behind the sofa. And Dash,

Leopold, and I braced ourselves. Into the Welcome Area came . . . *Sierra?*

"Good morning, my furry and feathered friends." She hung her bike helmet next to the leashes. "Are you ready?" she asked. "Because here comes . . ."

Cassie?

Cassie was followed by lots and lots of children, not to mention a few grown-ups, including Mom and Dad. Everyone crowded into the Welcome Area.

Cassie led me to a man holding a clipboard. "Mr. C., this is Coco," she said. "Coco, this is my teacher, Mr. C."

The man smiled at me. "I've heard so much about you, Coco," he said.

Then Cassie ran to stand on the bottom step.

"Welcome to Animal Inn," she cheered, "where we promise to love your pet as much as you do."

"Boys and girls," said Mr. C., "let's put on our best listening ears."

"How many of you have a pet at home?" Dad asked the students.

Several children raised their hands.

"Wonderful," said Mom. "Today you'll get a chance to meet the pets of Animal Inn."

Helena raised her hand. "I have a question," she said.

I had a question too. Was one of us still going to be . . . what was that word again?

Donated.

CHAPTER
12

Everyone made their way to the

party and play room. I chose a carpet square next
to Seiji. Cassie had said that Seiji could get a little
nervous. Maybe we could help each other. I was
feeling a little nervous too.

I turned in a circle, pawed at my carpet square,
and then plopped down. I tried to get comfy. No
use. I still felt nervous.

"Our first family pet was Dash," Mom told the class. She called Dash to the front of the room. "Dash is a Tibetan terrier."

Dash showed the class some tricks, like high-five and roll over.

"Now let's meet Leopold," said Dad. "His full name is Leopold Augustus Gonzalo Tyler. He's a scarlet macaw."

"Leopold is a pretty bird," squawked Leopold. "No, Leopold cannot believe it." Everyone laughed. Leopold took a bow.

"Our next pet is Coco," said Mom.

Cassie bounced over to my carpet square and gave me a big hug. "Coco is a chocolate Lab, but her favorite food is cheese," said Cassie.

"And all these pets love to listen to children read," said Dad.

"Yay!" cheered the children. "Let's read!"

Mom brought over the big cardboard box. She reached inside and took out a handful of books. She, Dad, and Sierra started passing them out to the children.

Hey, this was feeling just like Furry Pages. And I love Furry Pages.

I looked over at Dash. He was sitting in the middle of three children who were taking turns reading to him. Leopold was on his perch, paying close attention to a chapter book Mr. C. was reading aloud to a small group in the corner.

I took a deep breath. We had nothing to worry about. I was even getting my appetite back and my tummy told me it must be close to snack time.

Luckily, there were apple slices, crackers, and . . . *cheese*! Seiji gave me a piece of his. Yum.

After reading time, the class headed upstairs for a tour. We passed by the gerbiltorium to say hello to Fuzzy and Furry. How did they get hold of an apple slice?

We then went to the Reptile Room on the third floor. The turtle and snake enclosures didn't have any guests at the moment, but the children still enjoyed seeing the habitats.

We moved on to the Rodent Room, where there were two hamsters named Jackson and Wolfie, and a chinchilla named Morris. The children helped fill the food bowls and water bottles. Sierra told them a few fun facts about each animal. I didn't know that hamsters could store food in their cheeks. That was like having a snack-pack in your mouth.

In the Small Mammal Room, we met two checkered giant rabbits named Socks and Boots. Mom and Dad had the children sit in a circle. Then Sierra lifted the rabbits out of their hutch. She put them in the middle of the floor for a little bunny exercise.

It turned out Whiskers was correct. Lunch was right at noon. We all headed outside for a picnic.

Cassie's classmates were very generous with their sandwich crusts. Mom and Dad passed out cups of homemade lemonade. (I had water.)

And recess was right after lunch. The children's favorite game was Fishy, Fishy, Cross My Ocean. It was so much fun! I could see why this was Blub's favorite game.

After we cooled off and caught our breath, it was time to visit the barn and kennels. Everybody loved Toni the Angora goat, but Toni seemed a little concerned.

"Are there enough stalls for all these new guests?" she asked me.

"Oh, they're not guests," I said. "They're first graders."

Toni nodded. She looked relieved.

Before opening the door to the kennels, Mom

asked the children to be extra quiet. "We have a new guest named Lucky," she explained. "It's his first time here and he's a little homesick."

Lucky was resting on his bed. He still looked sad. I sure hoped his owner was coming back for him soon.

Finally, we returned to the party and play room for some coloring pages and crossword puzzles. One clue asked: *Which Animal Inn pet is the color of chocolate, but loves cheese? Four letters.*

I snuggled on my carpet square. I didn't feel nervous anymore. Just tired. School was a lot of fun, but it could sure tucker you out.

CHAPTER
13

The class gathered in the
Welcome Area to wait for the bus back to school.
Mr. C. asked for everyone's attention. I made sure
to put on my best listening ears.

"We need to thank Animal Inn for such a wonderful field trip," he said.

The children applauded.

"But the fun doesn't end here," said Mr. C.

It doesn't? I thought.

"Cassie's family has very kindly offered to donate one of the Animal Inn pets to our classroom."

"Yay!" The children all cheered.

Dash looked at Leopold. Leopold looked at Dash. Whiskers jumped into Seiji's lap.

In the middle of all the games and excitement and new friends, I had thought we were safe.

I noticed Dad walk toward Leopold's perch. It couldn't be Leopold. Could it?

"Here, Dash," called Mom. Was it Dash? How could it be Dash?

Then Cassie walked over to the sofa. Oh no! Was it Whiskers? Or was Cassie looking for Shadow?

Where was Shadow, anyway? I hadn't seen her all day.

"Coco," Mom said, looking straight at me.

 **283**

Gulp!

"Coco," Mom said again.

I couldn't believe what was happening!

"Coco, could you move over a little? Thanks."

Whew! I breathed a sigh of relief.

Mom walked past me and over to Blub's bowl.

"I'm sure your class will take excellent care of Blub until his owner returns for him," she said.

"And I think he'll be much happier in that beautiful aquarium in your classroom," said Dad.

"We are honored to have Blub join our school," said Mr. C.

"Yippee!" I heard Blub bubble happily. "I'm going back to school."

CHAPTER
14

Beep-beep!

Beep-beep!

"That's our bus," Mr. C. said. "See you tomorrow, Cassie!"

Cassie waved to all her friends. "Bye, Helena! Bye, Mattias! Bye, Lucy! Bye, Seiji! Bye, Arlen! Bye, Laura! Bye, everybody!"

"I'd better get going too," said Sierra. She

grabbed her bike helmet off the hook. "Thanks for inviting me. First grade beats college any day."

Cassie flopped down on the sofa. "Best field trip ever," she said with a happy sigh.

I couldn't agree more. Even Whiskers looked like he'd had fun.

Ding-dong!

"Who could that be?" asked Mom. She opened the front door.

It was Mr. C. He had his clipboard under one arm and Shadow under the other.

"The driver found her on the bus," he said with a smile. "She must have been riding around all day."

Mom thanked Mr. C. and waved good-bye. Shadow scampered behind the sofa.

"Shadow, where have you been?" Cassie said. "And where is your new collar?"

🐾 **287** 🐾

Ding-dong!

"Now who could that be?" Mom asked.

It was Lucky's owner, Mr. Patel.

"Sorry not to call first," he said. "But my conference ended early and I just couldn't wait to get back to Lucky. I hope it's okay if I pick him up today."

"He'll be happy to see you," said Mom. "I'll take you out to him now."

"I'll join you," said Dad.

"Me too," said Cassie. "I want to say hi to Toni."

I smiled. Lucky was going home.

Whiskers jumped up and peered over the back of the sofa. "Shadow!" he scolded. "Where have you been all day?"

Shadow strutted out. "All I can say, Little Brother, is—*best field trip ever.*"

EPILOGUE

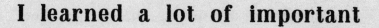

I learned a lot of important

lessons from our day with Cassie's class:

1. Lucky's name was a good fit for him after all.

2. Hamsters have snack-packs in their cheeks.

3. It's fun to be part of a school, whether you're

   a first grader or a fish.

4. Best field trip ever.

The next morning, after Jake, Ethan, and Cassie left for school, Mom and Dad got started on the chores around the inn. Soon Martha arrived to prep the grooming room. Her first customer was . . . *Sheila?*

Sheila had gotten a little too interested in a mud puddle, and was back for another shampoo.

"Hello, cuddly Coco," she whispered. "Nice to see you, wonderful Whiskers. Good morning, darling Dash. Greetings, lovely Leopold. Are you back there, shimmering Shadow? Hi there, beautiful . . . *Blub?* Hey, where's Blub?"

I told her all about Cassie's class visit and how Blub had joined their school. Sheila smiled.

That afternoon, Cassie came home carrying a big thank you card. Her classmates had drawn pictures on it.

"Look, Princess Coco," she said.

There was a drawing of Dash doing a high-five, and one of Leopold taking a bow. There was another of Cassie giving me a big hug, and one of Whiskers on the sofa. There was even a silly drawing of Shadow driving the school bus. Those kids sure had great imaginations.

Cassie opened the card to show me the inside. It said:

Thank you, Animal Inn.

We promise to love your pet as much as you do.

And underneath, there was a photo of Blub, happily swimming with all his new school friends.

DON'T MISS BOOK 4:
BRIGHT LIGHTS, BIG KITTY!

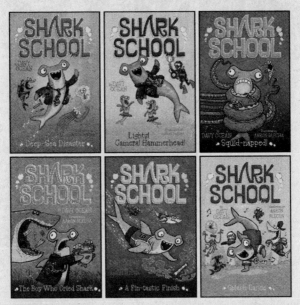

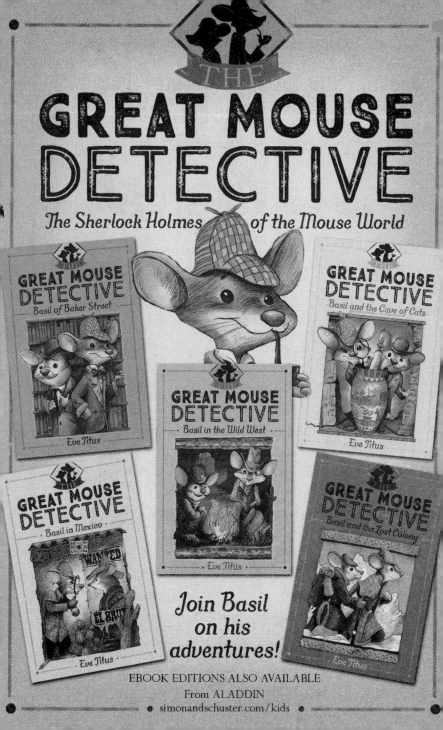

Join Willa and the Chincoteague ponies on their island adventures!